I0685832

THE GAME NIGHT

SARA LEA

THE GAME NIGHT

**I'M GOING TO MAKE THEM PAY.
NO MATTER WHAT.**

SARA LEA

Porkchop Publishing LLC
2709 N Hayden Island Drive STE 417603
Portland, OR 97217

For the ones who know my own darkest secrets.

For Le'mini for being my reason why.

For Jeremy listening to my endless monologues about books and writing.

Last, but not least, for all the paper straws that give me ideas.

THE INVITATION

8:23PM

JUSTIN: Dude, it was great bumping into you the other day. Glad you mentioned all of us should meet up sometime. I was also thinking it was time for a reunion. You in?

ALEX: um, sure. Sounds cool. What were you thinking?

JUSTIN: Maybe some drinks & a game night at my place next Friday?

ALEX: Game night? Still a nerd, huh?

9:12PM

ALEX: Dude? I was kidding. Sounds fine. Send me the address. You inviting everyone else?

JUSTIN: K great. And yeah. You got anyone else's number?

ALEX: I can let Lauren know. But I haven't been in contact with anyone else.

JUSTIN: K, cool man, I'll figure it out. Funny thing—I ran into Nick the day after I saw you. He thought it would be good to get together too but didn't want to do it at his place.

ALEX: Weird. I ran into Nick last week too. I'm surprised we've never run into each other before.

JUSTIN: True. 8pm next Friday? I'll send you my address.

ALEX: K.

9:25PM

ALEX: Hey sis, remember Justin?

LAUREN: um, from high school?

ALEX: Yup. Ran into him the other day. Just got a text from him. He wants to do a game night at his place next Friday.

LAUREN: WHAT?!

ALEX: Right? I mentioned we should get together, but I didn't think he would plan something just like that. He said it was time for the old gang to have a little reunion, but seems weird right?

LAUREN: Do you think something's up?

ALEX: IDK, but we gotta go.

LAUREN: IDK, Al, it's been 10 years.

ALEX: Exactly.

LAUREN: Ugh, fine, I'll ask Rich if he minds hanging out at home that night with Cody, but you owe me.

ALEX: Thanks sis. Give my nephew a hug from me. I'll send you the address.

9:32PM

JUSTIN: Hey man, it's Justin. Game night with the old gang at my house. 8pm next Friday. I'll send my address.

9:55PM

JUSTIN: Hello?

NICK: Justin?

JUSTIN: Yeah dude, it was so weird running into you last week. I mean, haven't seen any of you in years and then bam. Saw both you and Alex in the same week. You mentioned catching up, so figured we were overdue for a reunion.

NICK: Uh, okay, sounds good.

JUSTIN: Great, see you then. Sending address.

10:01PM

JUSTIN: Hey Lucy?

LUCY: Who is this?

JUSTIN: Oh sorry, it's Justin.

LUCY: Justin who?

JUSTIN: Cooledge. From high school.

LUCY: Oh.

LUCY: So, what's up?

JUSTIN: Hosting a game night for the old gang at my place next Friday at 8pm. I'll send you the address.

LUCY: Next Friday? IDK if I can...

JUSTIN: Everyone else is coming. Can't you figure something out? Come on, it'll be fun!

LUCY: um, I'll try.

JUSTIN: Great, see you then.

LET THE GAME BEGIN

1

L ucy leaned closer to the mirror, double checking her eyeliner and mascara. Straightening, she turned to the side and sucked in her already flat stomach. She cupped her small breasts, grimacing at their loss of perkiness. Although she was highly critical of herself, deep down she knew she looked perfectly fine. In fact, she looked good for twenty-eight. Still, she longed for the seventeen-year-old body that hadn't needed exercise and had easily forgiven those midnight burger runs. The one that hadn't been through a nightmare. That wasn't carrying the weight of a deep, dark secret.

Tearing herself away from the reflection, she smoothed the simple sweater she'd paired with jeans. She didn't want to look like she was trying too hard, but she was nervous. The thought of seeing her high school friends after so long made her queasy.

A hundred memories swirled around her mind. Did Alex hold a grudge? Was Nick still broody and handsome?

Flopping down on the couch in her small one-bedroom apartment, she picked up her phone and checked the time. She didn't want to get there too early. Her stomach churned as she propped her feet up and leaned back, clicking on Lauren's social media profile.

One by one, Lucy clicked through the pictures. Sure, Lauren was Alex's sister, but she'd also been Lucy's best friend for nearly three years... until their entire world came crashing down. In just one night, Lucy had lost everyone that meant everything to her. Barely eighteen and about to head off to college, it'd been nothing short of devastating. They'd had plans to share a dorm room, but Lauren chose to attend a different college altogether.

Despite the bitter way their friendship ended, Lucy had hoped they'd be able to put the past behind them one day.

Lucy focused on a photo of Lauren holding her son. *"Cody's first birthday."* Lucy focused on Lauren's face and zoomed in. Not a stitch of make-up, no filter, and somehow Lauren still had that ethereal look about her. Pale with dark hair and those Carolina blue eyes, she was stunning. Some overlooked it—after all, she had always been a little nerdy. With a short choppy hairstyle that had never been trendy, loose jeans and a plain t-shirt, she didn't need all the extras to stand out. She had a soft energy that drew people in. Like a fairy. She could have easily been an outcast with her love of anime, puzzles, and academic trivia. But there was an effortless quality to her that made her instantly likeable.

Lucy had always been a little jealous of that ease, but it was hard to dislike anything about Lauren. Besides, Lauren had always been more interested in books and art than attention. Even though she'd dated Justin in high school, Lauren wasn't like the other girls. She never seemed to have given it much thought, and she never made it seem like he was the love of her life.

"He's just a good friend," she'd always said. "Friends can date casually." She certainly hadn't been worried about leaving him to go off to college.

Lucy, on the other hand, completely overanalyzed things. At the time, she'd been so concerned about ending her relationship with Alex. Funny how anticlimactic it'd actually been compared to the rest of that horrific evening so long ago. But she hadn't been ready to give up on Lauren, even when the group decided never to speak again. Over the years, Lucy's resolve wavered, and she'd attempted to reach out. Lauren hadn't answered a single text or phone call and as much as it pained Lucy, she eventually moved on.

Not contacting Nick had been a lot easier. She was too ashamed of what she'd done.

Everything that went wrong that night started with me. It's my fault I lost the best friend I ever had. I deserved it.

She swallowed the lump in her throat.

But no. The real person to blame would be there tonight. Maybe this would be her chance to speak her truth.

Lucy closed her eyes and let herself go back to that night. A night she'd buried in the deepest, darkest corner of her mind. Divided into *before* and *after*, she saw every-thing leading up to it clear as day, but everything after that night was a blur, her mind and body numb. The moments when everything had turned for the worse stuck with her ten years later as clear as if it happened yesterday.

Lucy's stomach rolled as Alex realized what she'd done. Fighting to keep a clear head, she tried to think of an excuse, a reason, anything to make things better. The hurt on Alex's face was visible, and doom ballooned in her belly. She wanted to throw up. Alcohol fogged her mind, so much so that she barely squeaked out an apology which sounded completely insincere. What she had done—it wasn't Alex's fault. She and she alone had messed up. Alex might have been a bone-headed, immature teenage boy, but she had done something awful out of pure spite. Something to gloss over her real feelings.

Denying who she really was had cost them all so much.

The cheery ringtone startled her out of her thoughts, and she bolted upright. It was her mother. *Probably calling to remind me to eat dinner.* Lucy rolled her eyes and hit IGNORE before getting up to look in the mirror again. Her mother called far too often, concerned because Lucy wasn't married, wasn't even dating, and didn't really have any friends.

Lucy had tried all of that—friends and dating. But it never felt right. She'd faked it enough to survive college, but now she lived on her own, and despite working in a crowded office, she had no social life. She avoided connecting with anyone and declined invitations from coworkers. Eventually, they stopped asking.

She preferred to be alone. It was safe. She'd struggled

in college. It had taken time, but she managed to build a wall around herself and avoid relationships with too many personal questions.

A corked bottle—pressure building—she was terrified that one wrong move would cause her to explode.

The reflection in the mirror pulled her back. She cringed when she saw the way the sweater draped her hips. Was it the sweater or the jeans? She peeled the jeans off and pulled out a pair of slender dress pants reserved for meetings at work. No. She threw those back into the closet where they tumbled down the growing pile. Did she have any clothes left to try on?

Rifling through the drawers, she found the black designer jeans she'd spent an entire paycheck on. A size two, they'd been too snug the last time she tried them on, but maybe her rigid diet of black coffee and salads would finally pay off. Surely she would have lost a couple of pounds and could fit in them now…

She slid them on and smiled as they glided over her thighs and zipped up with little effort. Surprised, she glanced in the mirror sideways and realized they were now a little loose around the waist and baggy in the butt. Her shoulders slumped, and she sighed. There was just no winning. Resigned to looking like a fat, frumpy loser, she dug through her shoes until she found high-heeled boots. Rethinking, she tossed them back and grabbed canvas sneakers.

With plenty of time to kill, she perched herself on the edge of the couch, her leg bouncing. She checked the time on her phone again.

2

ONE HOUR BEFORE
GAME NIGHT

L auren ran a brush through her short hair and dabbed on some lip gloss. Glancing at her reflection, she frowned at the bags under her eyes. Her almost two-year-old son was going through a rough patch, and she hadn't had a full night of sleep in weeks.

"You look beautiful, as always." Lauren's husband, Rich, came up behind her and wrapped his arms around her waist.

Wrinkling her nose, she forced a smile. "Are you sure you're okay staying home with Cody?" Lauren asked again knowing Rich would never say no.

"Of course! Actually, Joel is coming over with Sammy so the kids can have cousin time."

"Oh, I didn't realize…" she said, eyeing the flowy top

and black leggings, her "mom uniform" as she called it. Normally, she didn't care about those things. But tonight, she knew she would be examined and judged as Lauren, not as Cody's mom.

She cleared her throat and met Rich's eyes in the mirror. "What time are they coming over?"

He dropped his chin to her shoulder. "They should be here anytime. Did you want to wait and say hello before you go?"

Scooting out of his embrace, she grabbed her sneakers and slipped them on before fumbling with her keys and purse. "Um, well, I just texted Alex that I would pick him up so I need to leave now." *There is no way I'm hanging around to face Joel.*

"Oh, okay, sorry, I didn't realize you were running behind," Rich said, his brows drawing together in confusion.

"Yeah, I mean, I'm not late or anything, but you know how Alex is. He's never ready on time, so I want to get there early enough to get him moving." Despite Lauren's forced laugh, Rich chuckled and nodded. *He's so easy to placate.* Too easy, really, which is how she'd ended up in this situation.

She hadn't actually made that plan with Alex yet, but facing Rich's brother was far less desirable than reuniting with the group of high school friends that had changed her life forever. She was forced to plaster on a fake smile at family gatherings and make excuses any other time Rich and Joel were getting together. So far, Rich had been oblivious, but how long could she keep it up? She dreaded the day when Rich noticed and confronted her. She didn't like lying, but what else could she do?

Rich sighed. "I'm glad you're picking him up, but you know, maybe you should bring up the drinking thing again with him. I don't like to stick my nose in, but I don't want him getting drunk at Cody's birthday party next weekend. A couple beers is fine, but I don't think I've seen him sober in months." Rich's face gave away nothing but concern. "I know you're worried, too."

She paused for a moment, her shoulders tensing. As worried as she was, she hated the idea of confronting him and using Cody as a pawn.

Rich hovered as she crouched to hug and kiss her son goodbye. Straightening, she turned to her husband.

"I keep bringing it up, but I don't want to completely push him away either, ya know?" They both knew it was a cop out.

Lauren was more than just a little worried about her brother. He'd always been a drinker. Even in high school. But back then it was little more than partying too hard on the weekends. Over the years, it had progressed. Now she suspected he was drinking during the day. Every day. He looked ragged.

She knew why; it was the same reason she'd made bad decisions, the same reason her relationship was a farce. They believed they didn't deserve to be happy. But how could she explain that to Rich? He didn't know about their past.

"I'll see you later." She stood on her tiptoes and gave Rich a quick peck on the lips.

"Have fun catching up with your old friends. Love you," Rich called out as he closed the door behind her.

Lauren hurried to her car and backed out of the drive-way. As she rounded the corner, she saw Joel's car turning onto their street. He waved, but she snapped her gaze back to the road as heat crawled up her neck. Pulling over, she grabbed her phone and dialed her brother's number.

"Hey, Laur," Alex answered.

The conversation was quick and much to her relief, Alex agreed to be picked up. His place was only ten minutes away, so she took a slight detour to collect her thoughts.

Before Alex invited her to this game night, she'd tried to avoid thinking about her old friends at all. But now, it seemed that every waking moment was consumed with the past.

Justin had been easy to date. He'd never pressured her, emotionally or physically. But she'd just been going through the motions. She wasn't even nervous to see him. It was Lucy, the person with whom she'd had the most attachment.

After that horrible night, Lauren had been crushed. To protect her brother, she'd done what she had to do and avoided them all. Even going as far as picking a different college. It'd been excruciating, especially losing Lucy.

She shoved aside the feelings of resentment. She'd been blaming everyone else for what happened, but that wasn't the whole truth. She knew she'd been partially responsible. Still, she hated them for what had happened.

That night had changed the trajectory of her whole life —not just because she'd been forced to attend a different college. She'd envisioned things blossoming with Lucy. It'd been wrong to pine for her brother's girlfriend, but it hadn't always been that way. Senior year, things had shifted. Her feelings had changed, and something made her think Lucy's had too.

A car honked, scaring Lauren into the present. Swerving, Lauren gulped in a ragged breath and squashed those thoughts down.

She was so angry... at all of them. There were days when she had fantasized about exposing the truth and blowing up their lives. But that would ruin hers too. There had to be a better way. Something she could do to get them to see what they had done. Somehow, she needed closure. Somehow, she had to move on.

What would it be like to see Lucy again? To hear her voice, the tinkling of her laugh. It'd been so long, and this might be her only chance.

Tonight wasn't just a reunion. Intuition had her nerves buzzing. The hair on the back of her neck stood straight up. She didn't know what she was capable of, but she knew she wouldn't leave without telling them they'd done wrong.

Lauren blamed all of them, even Lucy. Because of them, she'd lost the person she loved that night. Not to mention the future she had dreamed of through all of high school. *All of that, gone in a flash.*

3

"Are you sure I can't go with you?" Alicia whined in Nick's ear.

"I can't just show up with an uninvited guest," Nick answered, shrugging her hand off his shoulder.

"But I'm your fiance! Remember?" Alicia shoved her hand in his face, forcing him to look at the ring again. When she stuck her bottom lip out in a fake pout, he cringed and looked away with second-hand embarrassment.

The engagement had been a mistake—an accident, really. Henry, Nick's boss and Alicia's father, had pressured him to propose. Just as he had pressured Nick to date Alicia to begin with.

At first, Nick hadn't minded Alicia's company, even if she never knew when to shut up. She made up for it by being... *attentive*. But the feelings one should have for the person they were going to marry just weren't there. He hadn't had those deep feelings for anyone since high school.

Over time, Alicia had become clingy and demanding, and Nick found himself hoping she would get bored and move on. But her hooks were sunk in and her sights were set on a future with him. Nick couldn't understand why. Although he wasn't outwardly mean, he gave her the bare minimum.

He suspected it was because she'd never been told no. A spoiled brat and daddy's little girl, she'd never worked a day in her life. And maybe it was cruel, but the simple truth was that Alicia was homely. Oh she had the most expensive clothing, make-up, and hairstyles, but you couldn't change the structure of someone's face—at least not without major surgery. With small beady eyes, full cheeks, a pointy chin, and a tiny nose, she just wasn't attractive. A misshapen couch cushion with concave buttons.

But she had a fantastic body: large breasts and curvy hips. In the dark, Nick pretended she was someone else... The only other person he ever wanted to be naked with. Except it was getting harder and harder to fool himself.

At least he hadn't spent his own money on the ring. That was courtesy of Henry who had slipped it into Nick's dresser drawer with the 'premonition' Nick would find the right time to propose. Unfortunately, Henry had been right, in his way.

Nick peeled Alicia's hands off. "Not this time, sorry. I

don't even know why he wants us there. I won't be long. I just have to make an appearance, and then I'll head back home. Do you want to stay here tonight?" Nick offered, not wanting to hurt her. She hadn't done anything wrong. She was just the spoiled daughter of a rich prick. No one can pick their family. Even Nick knew that.

As he gathered his things, Nick couldn't shake the feeling that something wasn't quite right. Justin hadn't been his closest friend in high school. His sudden eagerness to reconnect was odd.

Was Justin's invitation some sort of attempt to mend the past? Or was there something deeper?

Had something happened? Did someone know their secret?

The unknown had been keeping him up at night. Every possible scenario ran through his mind. He just wanted to get it over with, but there was a nagging voice telling him that this reunion was more than it seemed.

True, he was bitter. He'd taken more of the blame that night than he should have. What he'd done might have broken the best friend code, but it'd been nothing more than high school drama. And it certainly didn't compare to the main event that night. It still bothered him that he'd let his friends bully him into silence, making him believe he was somehow at fault.

Unable to silence his curiosity, Nick grabbed his keys. *What was the worst that could happen?* He could just leave if things got too uncomfortable.

With a deep breath, he reminded himself that nothing would change the past. Maybe it was time to face it. Maybe tonight would finally bring them closure.

Maybe.

4

lex stood in front of the mirror and slicked his hair back one more time. His beard was scruffy, and at just twenty-eight, he already had lines around his eyes.

Why did I agree to go?

Game night? Justin had always been a little nerdy, but this sounded brutal. *Are we going to play fucking* Candyland *or what?* The whole thing sounded boring, but still he was curious to see everyone. And nervous. The acid in his stomach shot flames upward like a burning pit. He threw back some antacids and washed them down with a shot of whiskey.

It was so weird. If he had just gone home and ordered Chinese takeout like he'd planned, he could have avoided this entire situation. Seeing Justin had brought his life to a screeching halt. No amount of alcohol could drown the memories now. The second he locked eyes with Justin, everything had flooded back with a clarity so sharp, it was a wonder his mind hadn't shattered. Oddly enough, Justin wasn't the only one he'd run into recently.

It'll be interesting seeing Nick. Bumping into his old high school best friend had been awkward and surreal, especially right after seeing Justin. He couldn't even remember what they'd said to each other. The second he rounded the corner and saw Nick, all the blood had rushed to his head and pounded with the thunder of a thousand drums.

"Alex?"

Lost in his own thoughts, the sound of Nick's voice had made him jump, and he grabbed the cart handle to steady himself.

"Long time no see," Nick had added, his greeting filling the silence crackling between them.

Alex's hands shook as the morning's whiskey had begun to wear off. Time had stood still. Memories had flooded in, making him dizzy and nauseous.

The whole reason none of them had been able to talk to each other throughout the years was because of what Nick had done. It was Nick's fault. But Alex knew a judge wouldn't agree. Legally, Alex would take the fall.

Alex had somehow found it in himself to forgive Nick. As he got older, Alex realized he'd overreacted. Maybe he *was* to blame. At least a little. Or... maybe it was completely his fault for being a stupid, jealous idiot.

But no. He couldn't let himself admit that. The second he accepted that as fact, it was all over for him. He was already plummeting towards rock bottom. He didn't need something to push him off the edge of yet another cliff. Seeing Nick, though? That had been the reason he'd agreed to get together. Maybe after all this time, he wasn't the only one needing closure.

His phone vibrated in his pocket. Lauren's face appeared on the screen, and he answered. As sick as he felt, he would never ignore his own sister.

"Hey, Laur," he said, glancing at his jeans and noticing a stain on the thigh. He flopped down on his worn couch and looked around his living room. Distracted, his eyes roamed. A broken tv stand, scuff marks on the walls, the dingy rug. This wasn't the life he had planned, and he was embarrassed to think what he would tell his old friends.

Lauren's voice snapped him out of his thoughts. "Just making sure you're still going to this... thing."

"Yeah, yeah, I'm going. Are you still good to go? Is Rich okay with staying home with Cody tonight?" Alex smiled to himself thinking about his nephew, the brightest spot in his dismal life.

"Yeah, he's fine with it. Listen, should I pick you up?" Lauren asked, her tone careful. She left it unspoken, but Alex knew she figured he'd been drinking. She wasn't wrong. The whiskey hadn't been his first drink tonight. He glanced over at the counter and reminded himself to clean up the scattered beer cans and spilled liquor. He could only imagine how badly it smelled.

"Um... sure, that would be great to ride together," Alex answered, knowing he shouldn't get behind the wheel. And he certainly didn't want to show up in an Uber.

"Okay, perfect. Wear something decent. I'll be there soon," Lauren said, her tone stern.

Alex smiled despite himself.

Heaving himself off the couch, he went back to his bedroom and rummaged through his dresser for a clean pair of jeans that might still fit. He patted his growing gut and grunted as he pulled on a pair that barely buttoned. He'd been trying to cut back on fast food and takeout, but deep down he knew greasy food was only partly to blame. Especially since the majority of his diet was of the liquid variety.

For a beat, Alex considered not going. He normally didn't care what anyone thought, but seeing his high school girlfriend, Lucy, again filled him with emotions he couldn't quite figure out. *Stunning and fixated on always looking her best, she'll probably take one look at me and be disgusted.* Receding hairline, unkempt facial hair, deep lines on his face, growing gut… this wasn't what someone should look like before they even hit thirty, yet here he was.

Suddenly, he had the idea to look her up online. He didn't know why he hadn't thought of it before. A quick search brought him to her social media profile. It was private, but she had a couple of public photos. He scrolled through them quickly at first but then went back, methodically taking in every detail.

She was still beautiful, there was no disputing that. But there was something else, something he couldn't put his finger on. First of all, she had done away with her old look. No more skimpy outfits that showed off every inch of her body. Now she was fully covered in thick, loose layers. Had she simply matured?

Clicking back through, Alex noticed she looked particularly thin. In the most recent photos, her face was almost gaunt and dark circles ringed her eyes. *Is she sick?* She looked like his mother had when she'd gone through chemotherapy.

It was true that things had ended horribly between them, but even so, he didn't like the thought of her suffering or going through something like that.

She had the same last name, and there was no ring on her finger.

Maybe she's just as lonely as me.

5

FIFTEEN MINUTES BEFORE
GAME NIGHT

Justin arranged and rearranged the games on the oversized coffee table for the fifth time. His girlfriend Hannah was bustling around, setting up snacks in the kitchen. She closed the fridge again, no doubt taking out something else she had made. He was grateful she'd taken on the task of food and drinks, because he'd had no idea what to serve.

He'd been wanting this reunion to happen for so long, he almost couldn't believe it was going to happen. He checked his phone for the umpteenth time, making sure there were no cancellations. After ten years, he had a lot to get off his chest, and he needed all of them here for it.

But… what to do about Hannah? He hadn't even

considered that until just now. *Dammit.* He grunted, annoyed with himself.

He looked over the games. A couple of boring board games, a deck of cards, and charades.

They didn't matter; the night wasn't really about playing games. His anxiety was making him worry about mundane details. He wanted them all here so they could talk about what they had done. Now he had to figure out how they could do that with Hannah here. Maybe he could send her on a beer run. *Unfortunately, she overstocked everything so we wouldn't run out.*

A stab of pain caught his breath. Every day, the loss of Shane sat like a weight on his chest. He'd never had another best friend. Time hadn't eased that pain. That night had ruined his life.

"Justin, you can't just not go. I don't understand what happened," his mother had pleaded.

He'd just stared at her blankly, unable to give her the answers she wanted. His mind had been made up. He wasn't going to college. It was pointless. He didn't deserve a future that Shane would never have.

"I know it's been so hard for you after what happened with your friend. And breaking up with Lauren right after. This has been a horrible year for you." *His mother had attempted to soothe him, placing her hand on his arm.*

He'd felt her eyes on him, willing him to make eye contact, but he couldn't. If he did, he would crack. Every moment of every day was a risk—something was bound to break him. He could barely hold himself together. His mother had been in the dark about everything. It'd been so long since she'd known anything real about him. She hadn't even known that Shane was his best friend. Maybe his only real friend besides Lauren. Yet, he'd lost both.

"I've made up my mind. I already told them I'm not going. I told the store I was ready to go full-time. I'll just take a few classes at the community college." Numb, Justin's voice had been flat. He would go to work and come home, attend a couple of boring classes, nothing more. He wasn't even sure he could do that much, but he feared if he didn't, his mother would send him away for therapy. He would do whatever he had to do to avoid talking about his feelings.

"We should have bought some new games to play," Justin hollered to Hannah.

"Hm?" she asked, coming around the corner into the living room.

Justin tried to hide his disappointment. Instead of silky blonde waves cascading down her back, she'd pulled her hair back into a neat bun. With minimal makeup and a frumpy sweater, she looked more like a librarian than his hot fiancé.

"Do you need me to finish setting up any of the snacks so you can go get ready?" Justin asked.

"No, I'm ready," Hannah said.

"I've, uh, never seen you dress like this before." Justin tipped his head to the side and squinted. What was she playing at? Did she want his friends to think he dated frumpy chicks now?

"Oh… I just, I don't want your friends to think I'm trying too hard." Hannah blushed with embarrassment. "Should I change?"

"Nah, I'm not trying to impress any of them." Never a great liar, Justin's voice broke. He'd never wanted to impress a group of people more than he wanted to tonight.

"Uh, huh. I'll go put something else on. I wouldn't want you to be ashamed of me." Before Justin could argue, she quickly left the room.

His stomach flipped with guilt, and he reprimanded himself for being a douchebag. Sometimes he forgot how expressive his face was. He hadn't meant to hurt Hannah's feelings. But truthfully, he *did* want his friends to see his beautiful fiancé and be envious. He'd looked some of them up on social media and found Nick's girlfriend, in particular, was a real dog.

Justin flopped on the couch, checking his phone one more time. He wasn't expecting anyone for another fifteen minutes, but someone might show up early.

Leaning back, he rested his head and closed his eyes. He'd been avoiding thinking too much about this night and how it would feel to have the whole group in his living room. He'd planned the night as carefully as possible, considering every possible scenario and detail. But how could he know exactly what would happen?

Shane had been his best friend, maybe the only true friend he'd ever had. What happened that night had been horrific. For months, Justin hadn't been able to sleep. When it came time to head off to college and he backed out, his stepfather had been pissed.

Good old Coach Troy had been counting down the days until he could get Justin out from under his roof. But when Justin decided to stay in town instead, his mother had insisted he continue living at home to save money. He suspected she'd also wanted to keep an eye on him. Looking back, Justin realized his mood swings had been a dead giveaway that something more than the loss of a friend was going on.

Justin had even overheard his mother whispering to Troy about how she thought Justin was using *drugs*. The way she'd said it, he pictured her clutching her pearls. But Justin had never used drugs or even drank, other than the occasional beer. He'd never wanted to touch anything stronger than alcohol. Ever since that night, the thought of losing control was his biggest fear.

They *all* should have paid for that night. They *all* deserved to be punished.

Justin's hands clenched at his side. The familiar furnace of anger boiled up inside of him, something he'd pushed down over and over. When he bumped into Alex, it had taken him everything in his power not to unleash his anger on Alex. And though Nick was to blame too, he'd been more in control.

Justin forced himself to unclench his hands and rubbed his sweaty palms on his thighs. Tonight was the night he would finally fix what they had broken.

6

TEN MINUTES BEFORE
GAME NIGHT

ossing a pair of Justin's jeans to the side, Hannah frantically rifled through her small selection of clothes. She had recently moved in with Justin and didn't like clutter. Justin thought it was strange that she had such a meager wardrobe. But in her mind, all she needed were a few versatile, high quality pieces to mix and match.

Tonight, however, was about more than herself. It was about Justin. His friends. *Their* night. It was their time to reconnect. She wouldn't stand in the way of that, and the last thing she wanted was to draw attention to herself.

Her gaze flickered over the clothes she'd laid out—thoughtfully chosen, of course. She wanted to blend in, to not be a distraction, and to make sure everything flowed smoothly. Justin had seemed genuinely excited about tonight, and she couldn't bear the thought of it not living up to his expectations. This wasn't just about the games, or the food, or the cocktail she'd created with care; it was about making sure Justin and his friends felt welcome, comfortable, and above all, *entertained.*

Selecting the pair of black faux-leather pants, she eased into them. They gave off just the right vibe—edgy but understated, stylish but not trying too hard. They also felt better on her than they looked, and comfort was important. A glance in the mirror told her the sweater was still a safe choice. She needed to do her full face though, the exact way Justin liked it. Making quick work of it, the rhythm of her beauty routine and the practiced motions were second nature. One last glide over her hair to smooth her bun, and she took a calming breath, exhaling slowly.

She wanted everyone to feel relaxed, to play games and eat the snacks and rave about her signature cocktail. Justin had also blended some sort of frozen daiquiri, but secretly, she hoped they liked hers better. As she stood in front of the mirror, she found herself jittery just a bit with a mix of excitement and nerves.

She didn't need them to love her, but it would make the evening so much easier and go so much smoother if they at least *liked* her.

Selecting shoes was easier given she only had three pairs to choose from. She pulled the black ankle boots on, thankful she was tall and didn't wear heels, before giving herself a last once over in the mirror. Taking another breath, she camouflaged her nerves behind a carefully crafted mask.

This game night had thrown her for a loop. Ever since he'd invited his friends, Justin had been touchy, snapping at her and nitpicking her every move. She was determined to soothe his anxiety. If getting all dolled up put him at ease, she would do it. She'd done everything she could think of at this point. The night would be perfect. She would make sure of it. When it was over and they were all gone, she would be able to relax and feel like herself again.

7

FIVE MINUTES BEFORE
GAME NIGHT

etting everyone together in one night was a genius plan. It had taken me years to get to this point, waiting for the right moment to strike, but now my opportunity was rolling along all too easily.

All I had to do was plant one little idea.

The old gang was just living their lives like nothing had happened ten years ago, but I wanted to make them pay. For the choices they'd made, for the way they'd moved on, as if everything was fine, when I couldn't. They had no idea what was coming. But I was prepared. It was only fair, after all, since someone important to me—no, someone I had loved— had paid the ultimate price for their mistakes. For their negligence. For their silence!

I was certain they wondered why now, why get together

after so long. Their curiosity was a tool I had used well. I'd counted on it—their inability to resist the pull of the past.

Fear was my weapon. Fear would make them show up. It always did. The fear of facing consequences for their actions. The fear of being forced to confront the truth.

Smiling to myself, a cold satisfaction curled in my chest, and I leaned back in my chair.

It had been almost too easy. The invitations, the vague but compelling messages—little breadcrumbs to lure them all back for the ultimate reunion. They couldn't resist. How could they? The past wasn't something you could outrun, no matter how hard you tried.

I gripped the phone in my hand, staring at the screen as I scrolled through their social media accounts. They were all so good at pretending there wasn't a ghost of their past haunting their present. The part they'd played—chosen to play—didn't seem to bother them in the slightest. Why was I the only one racked with guilt? Unable to move on?

As far as they knew, I hadn't seen any of them in years. But I'd been watching all of them. After my life fell apart, it took me years to recover and pull myself together. But I couldn't let everyone get off scot-free.

Clicking through accounts, I ticked off every reason they deserved this.

Retribution.

Vengeance.

Justice.

Those stupid smiling faces with their families and significant others. Successful boasts about work and personal triumphs. Why should they be living the high life?

Did Shane ever cross any of their minds? Did they think about what we had all done? The part we had each contributed?

Did they even remember the blood on their hands?

The thought of them acting like nothing had changed, like they weren't responsible, caused my hand to tighten around my phone. They had no idea what this night would bring.

Tonight marked a pivotal moment. If I pulled it off, if I got them all in one room with no escape... At last, I'd be able to move on. The weight pressing on my chest would finally lift, and the ghosts of the past would dissipate. But there could be no mistakes. Failure wasn't an option. They had stolen so much from me already. This was the one thing in my control.

Clearing my search history with quick, deliberate movements, I erased any trace of my curiosity. I double-checked the time. Everything was in place.

They all thought they were untouchable. They thought they had gotten away with it. But tonight, they would learn how wrong they were.

Tonight was about consequences.

I stood up, savoring the rush of anticipation. Every muscle in my body was taut, ready for action. I could almost hear their voices in my head, their confusion, their panic.

It was time for everyone to learn a lesson.

No matter what.

8

THREE HOURS BEFORE
SENIOR PARTY

"Hey, babe, are you almost ready?"

Lucy tried not to roll her eyes at her boyfriend. For some reason, Alex was in a hurry to get to Chelsea's senior pre-graduation party, but it wasn't even nine o'clock yet.

"Oh yeah, I'm totally ready. You like my new hair accessory?" Sarcasm rolled off her tongue as she stepped into her bedroom with a section of hair wrapped around a curling iron.

Alex was sprawled across her bed playing a video game. His jeans were frayed at the bottom, his white socks gray and grungy. Lucy cringed.

"You look hot, you don't need to do all that," he absently commented, not bothering to look up.

She stomped back into the bathroom and let a long curl cascade down the thin spaghetti strap of her minidress. She smoothed a hand over the fabric, smiling as she turned side to side, admiring the way it clung to her body. She wasn't the smartest girl in the senior class, the richest, the nicest, the funniest, sportiest, or the most talented. None of that bothered her since she prided herself on being the hottest. At least, in her own opinion and that of half the senior class.

Twisting back and forth, she let her hands drop to her thighs where her fingertips grazed the bare skin. This dress was her shortest, but the material was so soft and stretchy it was comfortable. Even though it would probably ride up throughout the night as she danced with her friends, she put the thought out of her mind, not wanting to think about what pictures and videos might show up online the next day.

She turned to get a glimpse of the back of the dress—what little dress there *was* in the back—and her confidence soared. One thin strap held the top in place and the skirt dipped dangerously low, with just a small piece of material covering her butt cheeks. She would never admit it out loud, but looking at herself in the mirror turned her on. She felt mature and sexy. Soon, she'd be a college girl, flirting and flaunting her body around a college campus full of hotties. Alex and high school would soon be a distant memory.

It was funny how she had found Alex so hot when they'd first met. The new kid at Willow High their sophomore year, he'd been fresh meat. All the girls swooned over his smoldering brown eyes, dark messy hair, and square jaw. Lucy had expected him to be broody and deep. Instead, he'd quickly become the class clown and charmer. They'd started dating almost immediately while his twin sister, Lauren, quickly became Lucy's best friend. In fact, she liked Lauren even more than Alex. Maybe too much.

Definitely too much.

She pushed the thought out of her mind. Alex had a football scholarship to the state school and would be staying close to home. She and Lauren were going to the same college across the country and had signed up to share a dorm room. The thought gave her a thrill of hope. College would be the time to explore, not just those feelings, but so much more... and close to the top of the list was who she really wanted to be.

If she were being honest, she was really quite repulsed by Alex most of the time lately, but breaking up seemed pointless. She'd already decided to end things after graduation. No reason to rock the boat of their friend group now. Still, it was one of the biggest reasons she was looking forward to graduation.

Had she ever loved Alex? She'd thought so for over two years, but in the middle of senior year, she realized she had outgrown him. She was ready for something else.

Alex yelled at the video game and tossed the controller onto her fluffy area rug. Lucy rolled her eyes.

"So how much do you plan on drinking tonight?" She forced her voice to sound as casual as possible. More and more often, he'd get wasted and turn into a total asshole. Alex's drinking had gone well beyond simply letting loose and having fun.

"Don't need to worry about that, babe. Chelsea said we could totally crash at her house if we had too much to drink." As she walked back into the room, he reached for her, and tried to pull her onto his lap.

Lucy pulled away from him. "You'll wrinkle my dress." Her mind was elsewhere, thinking about what she had agreed to do tonight.

"Then take it off," Alex suggested with a wag of his eyebrows. He reached between her thighs and caught the fabric of her panties.

In the past, she would've laughed and climbed onto him, but lately he was getting on her nerves. His jerky "frat boy" attitude was old. She brushed his hand away, not caring that he looked miffed. To his credit, he didn't make any idiotic remarks.

"Can we at least agree not to do shots tonight? I know you want to drink and have a good time, but when we do shots, you get drunk so fast it ruins the rest of the night." Lucy turned to her closet to find a pair of shoes that she wouldn't hate wearing all night. She contemplated a pair of heels but almost immediately rejected them.

"I can handle a couple of shots, Luce," Alex said, rolling his eyes.

Lucy practically hissed. "I didn't say you couldn't. But a couple usually turns into more than you can handle."

"Stop trying to be my mom. It's such a turn off," Alex grumbled, reaching for his own shoes.

Lucy spun around. "I'm *not* trying to be your mom. And I don't care if it's a turn off. What's a turn off is how gross you get when you're drunk. Saying stupid shit, groping me in public, drooling and stumbling around and eventually puking… usually on someone's shoes! You have no control over yourself when you're like that, Alex, and I don't want it to ruin our last high school party. This is supposed to be the best night of the year! Chelsea's parents are gone, her whole house is open for us, and I don't want to have to babysit you or clean up your puke. I'm not the only one that's sick of it either!"

"What are you talking about?" Alex stood up from the bed, reaching for his keys on the floor.

"Um, Lauren and Nick and–" Lucy began ticking off names with her fingers, but Alex cut her off.

"Lauren's my sister. By default, she worries about everything. It's her job. And don't 'Nick' me. He's my best friend and is supposed to roast me. What do *you* know about Nick anyway?" Alex snapped, staring as though he expected an answer.

Annoyed, Lucy huffed and looked away, focusing on tying her shoes. The weight of his gaze pressed down on her, but she refused to look up. She'd already raised his suspicions—if nothing else, she'd just clued him in that she and Nick talked about him. She wondered what Alex was thinking. *What if he thought they had something going on?* She didn't have deep feelings for Nick, but she didn't want Alex to know what she really thought about him.

9

TWO HOURS BEFORE
SENIOR PARTY

Alex's phone dinged while Lucy shifted back and forth impatiently.

"Nick's here," Alex said before shooting a text back.

"Okay well, let's go then." Not waiting for a response, Lucy grabbed her mini backpack purse and pushed past Alex who followed but barely kept up. She swung the front door open and found Nick on the porch staring off into the distance.

"What are you looking at?" she asked, following his gaze. Alex stepped outside behind them, pulling the door shut.

"Watching those idiots." Nick tilted his chin towards a house on the corner where a few of Alex's football teammates were piling into a jeep, rowdy and acting like toddlers. Clearly some of them had already been drinking.

"Thought she was keeping it small," Nick said, shaking his head.

Alex shrugged and laughed. "She said it was okay if they came."

So, he'd been the one to invite the guffawing hyenas. Of course. It couldn't just be a small group of friends. Alex had to turn this into some beer-fueled jock fest. Lucy fought the disappointment creeping into her. *Do not let Alex ruin this night before it has even begun!*

The jeep pulled out of the driveway and peeled off, tires squealing, heading in the direction of Chelsea's house. Well, house was an understatement, but mansion didn't quite fit either. Mostly because it wasn't an old Victorian with multiple stories and sweeping ballrooms. But the house was spectacular; a contemporary style home with walls of windows and a fancy marble entrance and stairway.

"So, should I drive tonight? I can't drink anyway. I have to work in the morning..." Nick's gaze locked onto Lucy's for a second.

Her shoulders relaxed. It was going to be okay. "Great idea!" Lucy forced the enthusiasm, making Alex roll his eyes. But he just shrugged and tossed his car keys to Nick.

Lucy breathed a sigh of relief. *Thank god, one less thing to worry about.*

"Sure, you can drive, but we're taking my car. I don't want to ride with my knees around my ears." Alex laughed too loudly at his own joke. Alex drove his dad's hand-me-down SUV, whereas Nick's car could've practically fit *inside* the SUV, so he kind of had a point. But Nick was proud of the car he'd bought for himself and hated when Alex made wisecracks about it.

"Can we stop and get some french fries on the way? I cannot drink on an empty stomach," Lucy said, hauling herself into the backseat, not an easy feat at barely five feet tall and wearing such a skimpy dress.

Nick watched her climb in before jogging around to the driver side. He hopped in and turned the engine over as Alex got in the passenger side.

"Sure, babe, sure. Let's get you some fries. I could go for a burger right now. Wanna do the drive thru or go inside to eat?" Alex asked while Nick backed out of the driveway. There was no need to discuss where they'd go. Everyone would be at Lenny's, the local burger shack. Nothing but grease and salt, and they loved it.

"Inside. Lauren and Justin are supposed to stop by too," Lucy answered, fussing with her hair.

"They're still dating?" Nick asked, face scrunched.

"Dude, don't even get me started. My sister has some funky taste. I mean, don't get me wrong, Justin seems harmless. He's a total nerd, and that's cool, but he's just gotten… I don't know… different this year. Weirder somehow. I wish she would move on."

"Yeah, I used to like Justin, too. I think he's mixed up in some stuff," Lucy added, agreeing with Alex for once. She didn't want to tell Alex, but she was pretty sure Justin was selling drugs.

"I heard some rumors about that," Nick said. Lucy caught his eye in the rearview mirror, and they exchanged a knowing look, careful to tread lightly around Alex's "protective brother" mode.

Alex sat up straighter, his whole body taut with anticipation. Like a dog. "What'd you hear?

"Nothing specific really," Nick said, "just that he might be into pills or something. I don't know. Just gossip, ya know?"

"Yeah. I wish she would date someone normal, like maybe you!" Alex roared with laughter, causing Lucy to jump. She clamped her mouth shut and tried to hide her reaction.

Of course Lauren deserved someone better than Justin. But not Nick. Even if she was wrong in thinking it, she wanted both of them to herself. She refused to think about her best friend dating a guy she was attracted to. She had such mixed feelings about both of them, it would only lead to disaster. For her anyway. *What if they actually fell in love?* She pushed the thought away.

When Nick didn't respond, Alex looked at him sideways.

"Dude, you got nothing to say to that? I actually offered up my sister for you to date, and you don't jump on it."

"Ew, Alex, stop. They would be so mismatched," Lucy intervened, trying to save Nick from saying something stupid.

"Why do you say that? They both love me, so... it's perfect."

Lucy's eye roll was so exaggerated, her whole head moved. Alex and his big head were enough to make her nauseous.

"Look, Lauren's great, but I would never date my best friend's sister." Nick's voice cracked, and he glanced at Lucy in the rearview mirror. Their eyes met, but Nick snapped his gaze back to the road as they approached Lenny's.

Thankfully, Alex dropped it, and Lucy sighed with relief.

Over the roar of arcade games, laughter, and garbled conversation, Nick scanned the restaurant. Lenny's was always busy, but tonight was humming with the unparalleled excitement of seniors. The greasy smell of fries permeated the air with a thickness that their clothes would absorb and they would wear home.

"There's Lauren!" Lucy squealed, bouncing between them as she gave Alex and Nick's arms a quick squeeze. Nick swallowed hard as the tiny straps of her dress slipped. Forcing himself to look away, he followed Lucy's lead towards the table.

Lauren and Justin had somehow snatched the big corner booth. Alex weaved his way through the crowd and vaulted over the side of it, flopping onto the bench next to Lauren.

"Hey, sis!" He ruffled her hair until she grimaced and pushed him away.

Justin barely glanced up as he dove into his burger, grease dripping down his chin and landing on his shirt.

Lauren beamed at Lucy as she slid in beside Alex. "I ordered you some fries!"

Nick paused, looking at both sides of the booth. Finally, he squeezed in next to Lucy even though there was a lot more room on Justin's side. Lucy smiled at him, her eyes sparkling, before she turned back to Lauren, both of them becoming lost in excited chatter.

The buzz of the restaurant reached a breaking point as more kids packed inside. Soon, there were just as many seniors perched on the backs of the booths as in them. And at one point, Justin was forced to scoot closer to Lucy while someone slumped down on the already full bench.

When more food came, Alex dove in, ignoring everyone and everything around him.

Lucy turned to Nick and pushed her fries between them. "Do you want to share?"

"Oh, sure. Thanks," Nick said, grabbing a few without realizing how hot they were. Gasping, he chomped and swallowed before gulping down his soda.

Lucy's laugh tinkled in his ear as her hand landed on his thigh. "Are you okay?"

He chuckled and nodded, but he couldn't think of anything other than the weight of her hand on his thigh. Not knowing where to look, he mindlessly dropped his hands to his lap. Her fingers curled around his. His mouth went dry.

Despite the noise, all Nick could focus on was Lucy.

"Right, Nick?" Alex laughed loudly, reaching around Lucy and slapping Nick on the shoulder.

Nick jumped and Lucy snatched her hand back. "Uh, sure?" Nick answered. The crowd around them laughed so loudly he jumped again. Quickly recovering, he shrugged and joined them. Thankfully, everyone was oblivious. Lucy smirked and focused on eating her French fries.

Nervous, Nick glanced at Lauren who wasn't laughing

like the others. Sitting bone-straight, her gaze was fixed on Lucy with an intensity that gave him goosebumps. Something was off. His eyes darted back and forth between the girls, his heart pounding in his chest. The space between them shrunk. Her attention locked on Lucy, who appeared oblivious, Lauren still hadn't said a word. Nick's stomach churned, a wave of unease washing over him. He tried to act normal, but the tension in the air —whether real or imagined—was suffocating. Every second that passed felt like an eternity.

Was Lauren onto something? Did she know? His pulse raced. He forced himself to take a breath and prayed she wouldn't ask the question that would unravel everything.

This wasn't the way he wanted this night to go.

10

ONE MONTH BEFORE
SENIOR PARTY

"Thanks for coming over! I can't believe I am almost failing math again," Lucy said as she let Nick inside.

Butterflies swarmed her tummy, a mix of excitement and anxiety about seeing Nick alone. He was a much better distraction than Alex. Alex was... Alex. And Lauren's brother. She found herself thinking too deeply when she was with him. It was a situation she felt stuck in and got her mind racing. With Nick, she could just be herself.

"No problem. Anything for you." Nick smiled but caught himself when Lucy wrinkled her nose. "You know, anything for my best friend's girlfriend."

"Right. Well... I appreciate it," Lucy said, leading the

way into the dining room. "I set up here. I hope that's okay. And I grabbed us a couple cans of Coke and some chips."

"This is great." Nick dropped his backpack on the table and pulled up a chair. Lucy's notebook and textbook were open to the current assignment, and Nick visibly relaxed. Math had always been his comfort zone. Last year, Nick, Alex and Lucy had studied math together. This year, Alex wasn't taking advanced math, and when Lucy realized she was struggling and panicked, Alex had suggested Nick help her.

"Okay, so on this problem, it looks like you started out right, but here, you have to use this formula." Nick pointed to the textbook while Lucy grabbed her pencil.

They crouched over the notebook together, their foreheads almost touching while they worked through the next few problems.

"So, are you excited about going off to college in the fall?" Nick asked, his breath tickling the hair around Lucy's ears.

She froze, her pencil just above the paper. Until that moment, she'd been denying her physical response to his close proximity. A shiver raced down her back.

"Yeah, I am actually."

"Me too. You know, I'm only going to be like an hour away. We should hang out sometime." His voice softened, the implication hanging between them. So many meaningful glances had been exchanged, harmless brushing of their hands, standing closer than necessary. With all the different emotions kindling inside her, the last couple of months had been confusing.

Lucy didn't respond; she continued working on the

math problem, refusing to look up. When she made a mistake, Nick cleared his throat and leaned in to correct her.

"No, see you have to do this part first." Reaching for her pencil, his hand slid over hers and lingered a bit too long. She snapped her eyes to him, her breath catching. His face was mere centimeters away.

Nick's gaze fell to her lips. He swallowed.

Wetting her lips, her heartbeat thundered in her ears. "Nick…" Her voice was barely a whisper.

He leaned closer, their lips brushing in the gentlest touch.

Like a spark shocking her, Lucy jerked back, knocking her textbook off the table.

"I'm sorry. Lucy, I'm sorry!" Nick said as Lucy fumbled with the book.

"I think, um, I think I got it from here. Thanks so much for your help!" Lucy's voice cracked.

"We should talk about–" Nick started, but Lucy cut him off.

"It was an accident, don't worry about it. Let me walk you to the door." She grabbed his backpack and held it out to him.

His shoulders slumped, but he took the bag from her. "I'm good, I'll see myself out." But before leaving, he glanced back one more time.

Lucy rubbed her arms, wondering what she was going to do. Alex wasn't the boyfriend she wanted. In fact, she didn't want a boyfriend at all. She hated that she was attracted to these stupid boys.

Nick was supposed to be Alex's best friend, and Alex was one of the most popular boys in the senior class. She couldn't stop dating Alex to date Nick. They would be ostracized for it. She didn't even *want* to date Nick, but she couldn't stop thinking about touching him… kissing him.

She let out a frustrated groan and gathered her books before heading upstairs to her bedroom.

11

SENIOR PARTY

The drive to Chelsea's house was short. Justin and Lauren pulled up just as Nick, Alex, and Lucy were climbing out of the SUV. Giggling and talking over each other, Lauren and Lucy interlaced arms as they made their way up to the grand entrance.

Alex rang the doorbell, but thanks to the rhythmic thrum of the base coming from within, no one heard it. Shrugging, Alex grabbed the handle and swung the door open. They filed into the house, their shoes clattering across the gleaming marble floors. Elegant chandeliers bathed them in soft light, a stark contrast to the frenzied chaos of the party just beyond the foyer. A mass of students lounged on plush sofas and milled around the sleek, glass-topped bar. They wandered in together and Lauren soaked it all in. She was usually the one skipping out on parties, and she hadn't been to Chelsea's house before. She couldn't believe the set up. The kitchen island was littered with assorted bottles of liquor and ice buckets full of beer.

Double glass doors opened to the enormous yard where a shimmering pool reflected the stars. Beyond the crackling bonfire, fairy lights struggled to break through the smoky air. Everything about the evening felt like a scene from a movie. *Finally, I'm at one of those stereotypical high school parties.* Lauren didn't know if she was proud of herself for showing up to experience it at least once, or ashamed of herself for caving.

Alex was quick to grab a drink just as Chelsea bounded up to them.

"Hey, you guys!" She giggled and hiccuped, sloshing her drink.

Lauren and Lucy gave her quick hugs while Alex and Nick wandered off into the sea of faces.

"I love your outfit!" Lucy said, admiring Chelsea's floral halter top and tight white mini skirt that barely covered her fluorescent orange bikini.

"Same, girl, same!" Chelsea appraised Lucy, and then gave Lauren an awkward smile.

Unconcerned about her bland outfit of wide-legged jeans and a graphic tee featuring an outdated band, Lauren ignored her. She wasn't expecting compliments. It certainly wasn't why she had dressed this way.

"Well, there's a ton of food in the kitchen—my parents made me promise to make sure no one drank on an empty stomach—and of course, there's anything you could imagine drinking. Feel free to help yourself!"

Chelsea emptied her drink in one gulp then raised her hands up and danced away from them.

Justin leaned close, his lips brushing Lauren's ear. "I'm going to look for Shane."

She nodded, fine with Justin ditching her to hang with his friend. She was more interested in hanging out with Lucy and making the best memories with her tonight anyway.

But before she could focus on having fun, she needed to make sure Alex wasn't going to get completely obliterated. Even though they'd just eaten at Lenny's, she went in search of a snack and to make sure Alex ate something else. She didn't want to babysit her brother all night, and she'd found that plying him with an exorbitant amount of food tended to keep his drunken beast happy. Or at least *happier*.

Lauren grabbed Lucy's hand and dragged her along. Alex was already perched on one of the counters, a beer in hand and a bottle of tequila next to him. Nick was leaning against another counter, his arms crossed, looking bored.

"Who wants to do shots?" Alex shouted, waving his hand while grabbing the bottle of tequila with the other.

When a slow line began to form, he shouted louder, "Come on, don't be shy! Step right up!" One by one, they marched by him, tilting their heads back and letting him pour directly into their mouths.

Lauren shook her head as she gathered a plate of food and brought it over to Alex.

Confused, he looked at her but then grabbed a sandwich and took a huge bite. "You know I just ate, right, Laur?" Alex said around the mouthful.

"Yeah, but so what? When do you ever stop eating?"

Alex threw his head back and laughed. "True. Cheers!" Alex raised a beer and chugged it.

Students flowed in and out of the kitchen, drinking, snacking, and dancing. Lauren kept an eye on Alex while Lucy chattered on next to her. Lauren struggled to focus between Lucy's bubbly voice and her brother's drunken exploits.

Finally, when she was satisfied that he was pacing himself, she touched Lucy's arm and leaned in. "I'm going to find Justin and check in really quick. You good in here for now with Alex?"

Lucy smiled and nodded, but something flashed over her face quickly. It was enough to make Lauren pause.

Was Lucy just bummed that her best friend was going to hang out with her boyfriend, or was there something else?

"I'll be quick, I promise," she said, squeezing Lucy's arm. Lucy still looked disappointed but didn't argue.

Before Lauren could question it further, Lucy's attention turned towards Alex and another football player arm wrestling.

Pushing her questions to the back of her mind, Lauren slipped out of the kitchen. She wove her way down a hallway and through the front living room, scanning the crowd. As she tried to squeeze by a couple of drunken seniors dancing close, a familiar voice called out over the noise.

"Hey, Lauren!"

Lauren grimaced as she came face-to-face with Shane's girlfriend, Hazel. Hazel was annoying and clingy, but Lauren felt bad for her. She didn't seem to have any actual friends.

Hiding a groan, she greeted Hazel. "Hey."

"I can't believe you guys are graduating in two weeks!" Hazel squealed and clung to Lauren's arm with the death grip of a cat trying to get out of the bathtub.

"And you'll be a senior!" Lauren shouted back, nodding to the music while trying to figure out how to move the conversation along as quickly as possible. "Have you seen Justin?"

"No, I haven't. I was looking for Shane. Haven't seen either of them." Hazel sounded uninterested, standing on her tiptoes, eyes roaming over the crowd.

"Okay, well, if I find them first, I'll tell Shane you're looking for him!" Lauren didn't wait for a response before slinking away. Just before she slipped out of the room, she looked back and caught a glimpse of Hazel standing by herself. Hazel raised her glass to Lauren and shot her a forced smile. Lauren nearly went back, but then she reminded herself it wasn't her job to save every stray.

12

GAME NIGHT

"Well, this is it."

Lauren parked and double checked the address on her phone. She and Alex sat in the car, neither wanting to make the first move to get out. The house was a small ranch on a quiet street with a tall privacy fence wrapping around to the back.

"I'm not sure what I expected, but–" Lauren's eyes wandered over the property. It was small and neat and… very mundane.

"But this isn't it!" Alex finished, wiping his sweaty palms on his pants.

"Right?" Grateful she wasn't the only one who thought it was odd, relief poured out of her. Although, she couldn't quite explain why. She just hadn't imagined Justin living in a place so… normal. An apartment in a shady neighborhood, sure. An upscale penthouse? Why not? But not the scene of a family sitcom.

Another car pulled up behind them, and Lauren glanced in her rearview mirror. "That must be Nick."

Alex turned, trying to get a glance of the driver. "Yep, looks like it. I guess we should get out," Alex said, but neither of them reached for their door handle. The crunch of more tires pulling up made them turn their heads. Lauren's stomach did a flip when she saw Lucy in the driver's seat.

"I guess that's all of us," Alex said with a sigh, reaching for his car door.

Lauren's legs wobbled like jelly as she climbed out of the car.

Nick was next to hop out. He dropped his keys and fumbled around in the dim light to find them.

"Good stall tactic, Nick," Lauren muttered, turning and watching Lucy exit her car.

Lauren swallowed and took a couple steps, unsure how to read the serious woman. There was very little trace of the once curvy, bubbly girl. Every move was calculated, intentional, careful. And she was thinner than Lauren had ever seen her, almost twiglike.

Lucy closed the gap between them, her face giving nothing away. Memories swam in Lauren's mind, a silent movie replaying every smile, every laugh, every secret shared.

Just when Lauren thought she couldn't stand another tense second, Lucy's cold demeanor shattered. A sob escaped her, her body visibly relaxed, and she hurled herself into Lauren's arms.

Lauren slowly tightened her embrace, her hand

brushing the back of Lucy's hair. With another breath, her shoulders began to shake. Tears sprang from her eyes and streamed down her face. "Wow. I can't believe I'm seeing you."

Lauren stepped back and locked eyes with Lucy.

Alex cleared his throat, shaking them out of their stupor.

"Sorry, it's just when you finally see your best friend after so long..." Lucy's face flushed. Lauren glanced at Alex and Nick. The guys exchanged a quick glance, and Nick shrugged.

"Well, uh, it's good to see you both," Alex said, slapping Nick on the arm and giving Lucy a quick nod.

Lauren exhaled a laugh and shook her head. "We should go inside. Justin probably thinks we're having the party on the street."

They made their way up to the door in silence. She wasn't sure how the others felt, but nervous energy tingled underneath Lauren's skin.

What are we doing here?

13

SENIOR PARTY

Lauren found Justin sitting by himself in a corner of the living room. "Hey, there you are!" She offered him the brownie she'd been carrying around.

"Thanks," he shouted over the music and took a huge bite. "This is good."

"Let's go outside," Lauren suggested, leading the way out to the patio. Several kids were sitting on the pool ledge, legs dangled in the water. Surprisingly, no one had jumped in yet. It was only somewhat quieter outside, but they found a loveseat in a corner to relax on.

Justin's usual goofy energy was subdued, his gaze fixed on something in the distance.

Lauren noticed. In fact, she'd been noticing how he

avoided eye contact lately and avoided being alone with her.

"You've been acting weird lately," she said, crossing her arms and narrowing her eyes. "What's going on?"

Justin looked around the patio as though searching for an escape. The music seemed to get louder before he responded. "Nothing, L," he said casually, but it didn't fool her.

"Don't do that thing, Justin. Don't shut me out. You've been acting weird for months. You can tell me anything." She nudged him with her elbow. Even before they dated, they were good friends. She thought they were pretty open with each other. *What is going on with him?*

He shifted and refused to look her in the eye. Lauren reached over and slipped her hand into his, her fingers looping between his. "Tell me," she urged, her tone gentle but unrelenting.

Justin's sigh was heavy, and he ran a hand through his curly hair. Finally, he answered, his voice low enough that Lauren had to lean in.

"I've been dealing pills." Justin looked almost as shocked by his admission as Lauren felt.

"*What?*" Springing upright, Lauren shook her head in disbelief. She yanked her hand from his and glanced around to make sure no one was lingering nearby. Justin's head fell forward until his chin rested on his chest.

"I don't believe it," Lauren hissed, her stomach turning. "Where are you getting them? *How* are you getting them?"

After a long pause, Justin blew air out between his lips. "Troy. Coach Troy. He's the one giving them to me."

"*Coach Troy?*" she gasped, quickly lowering her voice.

"As in your *stepdad* Coach Troy? He's giving you pills? Where is *he* getting them?"

Justin nodded in response but just stared at the ground between his feet. He still refused to meet her gaze. "Yeah, he's not exactly giving them to me... but he knows. He doesn't care. I mean, well, it's complicated. I'm not really sure what he was doing with them. But I saw them one day when I was in his office, and I was just curious at first. There were just so many–" Justin stopped, his thoughts carried away by the wind.

Lauren's mind raced, trying to figure out what else Justin was hiding. Coach Troy was strict, certainly not the "be your best friend" type of coach. He had always been such a hard-ass running the football team. He acted like everything was life or death. How could he be complicit in this? No. Not complicit. The perpetrator! There was no way.

"Why would he be letting you do this? Helping, even?" Her voice rose an octave.

"I know. It sounds crazy, but um, well, the thing is… one day, I walked in on him." Justin's voice cracked and he paused, balling his fists so tight, his knuckles turned white.

"Walked in on him doing what?" Lauren shrieked. Justin's head snapped up, and he looked around anxiously.

"*Shhh!*" he admonished her. "I walked in on him doing… something he didn't want to get caught doing. So, he's stuck. Because I know his big secret. He can't turn me in for taking his pills, because then he'd get caught too."

Horrified, a thousand terrible scenarios flashing through her thoughts, Lauren's eyes grew into saucers. "What was he doing? Wait, don't tell me. I feel sick."

Lauren pulled her knees up to her chest and wrapped her arms around her legs.

"You don't want to know, but it doesn't matter. I can't say anything because I'd get caught, and he can't turn me in because he'd get caught. So, we're in it together now, whether we want to be or not."

Lauren's stomach churned, the bitter taste of acid on her tongue. It was all too much to process. Her boyfriend, a *drug dealer*? His stepfather, doing who knows what…

Her brain short-circuited—Justin had some horrible knowledge of his stepdad, and he felt he couldn't do anything. She snuck a glance over and found Justin rubbing the palm of his hands over his eyes. Her heart clenched. It explained everything. Why he'd been acting weird, why his grades had dropped… everything. Sure, he was doing something he shouldn't but to be trapped with this secret?

Before she could say anything else, Justin's best friend Shane sauntered out onto the patio.

"Hey, you two. Busy?" he joked, hinting that they might still want to be alone.

Justin used the chance to escape and hopped up. "Naw, I was hoping you'd make it tonight!" Justin forced cheerfulness through his words and slapped Shane on the back.

"I'm gonna go grab a beer and some chips. You good, L?" Justin turned back and looked at her. She just sat there, numb and nodding.

Finally, she lifted a hand to wave them on. "You guys go on and catch up. I'm just gonna hang out here for a bit." She smiled for Shane's sake.

They left her staring at the crisp blue pool water, weighed down by Justin's admission.

14

J ustin crept down the empty hallway, his gaze focused on Coach Troy's office door. The chance he was taking made all the other risks seem like child's play. Still, the spare key was burning its impression into the palm of his hand.

For the past month, he'd been stealing pills from his stepdad, who had both his own medication and that of a few students stashed in his office. Despite making a copy of the key and returning it without being detected, Coach Troy had caught on.

A week ago, he'd been about to knock on his mother's bedroom door to ask about having Shane over for dinner, but the tone of her voice had made his hand freeze midair, recognizing her barely controlled anger.

"What makes you think Justin's involved?"

"Listen Julie, I'm not accusing him of anything. Yet. I'm just letting you know that a lot of pills are missing. No one else has access to my office. And there are rumors."

"What rumors? That Justin is using? He seems totally normal.'

Coach's voice rumbled to a low whisper. "I wasn't going to come to you until I actually had some sort of proof, but I've heard he's been... selling pills."

"Selling pills? You're accusing my son of dealing drugs?"

Coach Troy had shushed her. "I don't know. Maybe."

Unable to hear the coach whispering, Justin had put his ear to the door and heard his mother crying.

Between sobs, she had choked out, "I really hoped I would never have to choose between you and Justin, but if it comes to that, I'm going to choose him."

"And just what does that mean?"

"He's my son! I'll do whatever I need to do to protect him."

"Even if he's the one stealing the pills? What if he's selling them? What then?" Coach had asked, defeated.

"I just can't believe that's true. So you had better find out who it is and have solid proof. Period. I don't want to hear any more accusations based on rumors from some meathead football players."

Julie's anger could be as poisonous as venom, and Justin swallowed hard as he had inched away from the door. Fortunately he was not the one on the other side of her wrath.

The last thing he'd heard Coach Troy say was, "Meathead football players? Tell me how you really feel, Julie."

So, why was he taking such a huge risk now? Because of Braden Watkins. Braden Watkins, one of those meat-head football players, was threatening Justin if he didn't get him more pills.

Justin stood in the school hallway glancing both ways, trying to act nonchalant. That morning he'd overheard Coach telling his mother that he had an appointment after school and would be home late. The darkness from behind the small frosted window confirmed Coach wasn't inside.

Justin had once made the mistake of entering through the boys' locker room. It'd been too easy, especially since both doors used the same key, but just as he had slid the key in, a couple of students burst in after using the track for a run. He'd had to yank the key out and hide in one of the stalls. After that, he'd been too nervous to go in that way again.

The hallway was safer. He could keep track of when Coach wouldn't be around and slip in and out.

The key stuck to his sweaty palms as he glanced over his shoulder again. Inserting it into the lock, he slipped inside. He closed the door with nothing more than a soft click and stood frozen.

Along the short wall of the L-shaped office was a small storage cabinet and desk. The longer wall held a loveseat and wide cabinet. The door leading to the boys locker room was in back.

Fueled by adrenaline, his heart raced. His pulse pounded in his ears, the beats drowning out his thoughts. The office was quiet, magnifying the echo of his shallow breath.

But then a muffled sound broke through the silence,

sending a chill down his spine. A low moan followed by whispered protests. He stopped in his tracks, his eyes darting around, trying to locate the source of the noise.

He stepped closer, his feet moving without thought. The space between the tall cabinet and the wall was just wide enough for him to peer through.

His breath caught.

A familiar figure was crouched over a girl, her back pressed against the loveseat. The dim light from the office hardly illuminated the scene, but it was enough to make out the girl's disheveled appearance and tear-streaked face. Justin's stomach turned.

As he began to process what was happening, the football on top of the cabinet rolled off and hit the ground.

Coach Troy jumped away from the girl on the sofa and yanked his pants up. "Who's there?" His voice cut through the air like a knife, and he locked eyes with Justin.

In that moment, Justin saw something he hadn't expected. It wasn't anger but fear.

Justin didn't move, couldn't even breathe. His heart pounded, threatening to jump out of his chest, as he stared at his step-father. Everything inside him screamed to run, to turn around and forget this ever happened. But he couldn't. He couldn't walk away. Not from this. He had something on Coach Troy that could destroy him.

Troy closed the gap between them in three long strides. He blocked Justin's view of the girl on the couch, but it didn't matter. The image was burned into Justin's mind. She looked familiar, but he couldn't put a name to the face. She must have been a student in a lower grade, because she definitely wasn't part of their senior class. Justin's stomach lurched.

"What are you doing here?" There was an edge to Coach's voice, something dangerous.

Justin's mouth went dry, but he forced himself to speak. "What are *you* doing here?"

Troy's gaze hardened, but the man's stoic expression cracked, and Justin saw a flicker of something deeper—guilt, or shame, or maybe even regret. It was hard to say.

"Never mind," Troy muttered, tugging a hand through his hair. His eyes darkened. "I think I know exactly what you're doing here. The question is—what do you think you've seen?"

Justin didn't know how to respond. His mind was a whirlwind of thoughts and emotions. His chest tightened, and for a brief second, he considered walking out. But he couldn't pretend nothing had happened. Something about the scene—the girl, the panic in Coach Troy's eyes—kept him rooted to the spot.

"What do you mean?" Justin's voice was steady, his resolve firm. He wasn't one to stand up and fight for injustice, but this crossed a line even he couldn't ignore.

His step-father's eyes narrowed. "It's simple," he said, his voice low and strained. "You walk away. You forget this ever happened. And I do the same. Understand?"

But Justin didn't understand. Walk away? He couldn't. Not when the girl's face, stained with tears, was still seared into his mind. "How can I just forget?" Justin asked, his voice rising. "What's going on here? Who is she?"

The coach's features twisted in anger, a flicker of something darker crossing his face. He took a measured breath.

"She's none of your concern." His words carried the weight of someone who knew how dangerous the truth could be. "Get out of here, Justin. This is none of your business. And I will make sure no one knows what you have been up to. Especially your mother." Coach gestured toward the cabinet with his chin.

The easy choice was to walk away and pretend he hadn't seen anything. But the harder choice—the choice that would change everything—was to stay. To confront the truth. But it would also mean a lot of trouble for him.

Without looking away, Justin straightened his spine. "What if I don't leave?"

Panic flickered across Troy's face. Then, just as quickly, it was replaced by something else, something colder. "Then you'll regret it."

The warning made Justin flinch. The decision was made.

He swallowed hard before turning and leaving, refusing to acknowledge that he'd just sacrificed some girl, and who knows how many others. All for his own selfish sake and his mother, who was married to this monster.

Running from the school, Justin jumped into his beat-up car and slumped over the steering wheel. He gulped in air, willing himself not to throw up, realizing that, regardless of the choice he just made, life as he knew it was over.

15

GAME NIGHT

All four of them took a step back as they realized it wasn't Justin answering the door. Lucy squinted under the dim porch light. It was hard to see the person's face through the cracked door, but it was definitely a woman.

Lauren was the first to speak up. "Oh my gosh, we're so sorry. This must be the wrong house!"

Unable to find her own words, Lucy closed her mouth and gave Lauren a grateful smile. Lauren fumbled with her phone and scrolled until she found the address Justin had sent.

Was this some kind of joke? It seemed unlikely that Justin would be pulling one of his old high school pranks after all this time.

Nick had already stepped off the porch and was

backing away towards his car; even in the dark, Lucy could tell he was embarrassed.

"We're really sorry to bother you," Alex said, tugging Lauren's arm. "We must have gotten the address mixed up."

When Lucy turned to follow them, the woman opened the door further. "Wait!"

Stopping in her tracks, Lucy turned around, wondering what this woman could possibly want. She took in her appearance— hair in a perfect bun, flawless makeup with bright red lipstick, and a casual outfit that probably took longer to throw together than it should have. Lucy shrunk into herself, suddenly ashamed that she hadn't spent more than a couple of minutes getting ready.

"I'm Hannah!" the woman announced. But when the group shared a puzzled look, a flash of irritation crossed her face before she quickly composed herself. "Justin didn't tell you? I'm his girlfriend. Welcome! Please, come in." She gestured behind her and opened the door wider, stepping back to allow them in.

That's awkward. Justin didn't invite us here to rehash the past? Lucy wondered why he hadn't mentioned that his girlfriend would be there.

At that moment, Justin popped his head around the doorframe, and Lucy's shoulders relaxed. So it wasn't just some joke. The realization of that brought both a flood of relief and a wave of anxiety.

"Hey guys, sorry! I was just mixing some drinks for everyone." Justin smiled.

Hannah whipped her head around. "I already made cocktails," she snapped, but then she seemed to catch herself and forced a smile.

Justin let out a nervous chuckle. "I know, but I just wanted to make something in our high school color—red! Your drink is blue, but it's okay, we'll drink that too." He reached over and rubbed her arm.

"Yeah, don't worry, we'll drink both!" Alex confirmed with a transparent attempt to divert the awkwardness.

"I'm sure you will," Lucy muttered under her breath. Alex didn't seem to notice, but Hannah did, and she raised an eyebrow. Lucy shifted her eyes away. She needed to be more careful about her reactions tonight. Alex might not be paying attention, but clearly others were.

"Dude, this den is pretty kick-ass." Alex roared with laughter, sounding more like his high school self than ever. In fact, Lucy noticed they all seemed to fall back into their old roles. Lauren was actively watching Alex with a careful eye. Nick was silently taking it all in. Justin was in his own world, and Lucy was already feeling annoyed by him.

"So, you're the ex-girlfriend," Hannah teased Lauren with a quick laugh.

Lauren chuckled, her eyes flicking to Justin. "I guess so. But I'm happily married with a son, so don't worry, I'm not here to steal him back," Lauren joked, her snort giving away how uncomfortable she was.

Lucy smiled to herself, a warm fuzzy feeling blooming in her belly witnessing how little Lauren had changed.

Hannah's barking laugh made them jump. "Sorry," Hannah said, covering her mouth. "You're funny, and I'm nervous. I don't want Justin's old friends to hate me."

With that admission, the tension in the room eased like a balloon releasing air.

Lucy watched the interaction with mild amusement, but she struggled to tear her eyes off Lauren.

"There is a ton of food and drinks in the kitchen," Hannah offered. "Please, feel free to head in there and grab whatever you want. Make yourselves completely at home."

Alex hopped out of the leather recliner he'd slumped in. "I'm definitely having one of those cocktails!"

Nick glanced at his phone, and Justin cleared his throat.

"I was thinking, maybe we should ditch the phones tonight," Justin suggested.

Nick paused, and eyed Justin curiously.

"It's just... I thought..." Justin started but Hannah rescued him.

"It was my idea." Her smile was bright. "I recently had a girls' night out with some old sorority sisters, and they had us leave our phones in a bowl. It made the night *so* much better. Without our phones, no one could dodge truly reconnecting."

Justin whirled around and pursed his lips. It appeared as though he was about to say something but thought better of it.

Interesting, Lucy thought.

"Uh, sure," Nick said, silencing his phone and dropping it into the basket Hannah produced.

Hannah turned to Lucy and Lauren and nudged the basket towards them. "What do you say?" she asked, tossing her cell in. Justin pulled his out of his back pocket, powered it off, and dropped it in.

"I guess, sure," Lucy said, following suit. She had no one to text or call anyway.

Lauren tried to smile, but it was more of a grimace. "Well, um, what if my husband calls? I have a toddler... I mean, he would never call unless it was an emergency, but if something happens I don't want to be unreachable." Lauren held her phone in a death grip.

"Oh, no worries, just turn your volume up. If it rings, we will know it's yours, and you can get it."

Defeated, Lauren hesitated a moment longer before dropping it in with the others.

Alex came back from the kitchen carrying a huge cup of the red drink Justin had made. "Dude this is damn good. What did you put in here? It tastes like candy." Alex slurped, an obnoxious sound.

Cringing, Lucy caught herself and fixed her face, but she felt someone watching her. Glancing around, she found Nick staring. He gave a curt nod and smiled. Lucy smiled back, relieved that her disgust was witnessed only by Nick.

"We're putting our phones in this basket for a device-free night," Lauren told Alex, gesturing towards the basket.

"Oh sure, I'd rather work doesn't call me anyway." Alex silenced his phone and added it to the others.

"Great! I'll just put this out here on the table in the entryway. It'll be easy to hear from the den, don't worry," Hannah reassured Lauren as she slipped into the hallway.

Justin clapped his hands and gestured to the kitchen. "Alright then. Why don't we all grab a drink and some snacks before we get comfortable out here? We can catch up and what not before we play a few games."

16

SENIOR PARTY

Justin and Shane wandered back into the house together and stopped in the kitchen. Shane grabbed a can of soda and one of the fancy deli sandwiches off a tray. Justin grabbed another brownie, and then they pushed their way back through the growing crowd, kicking plastic cups out of their way.

"Shane!" A goth girl burst through the mob, throwing her arms around him.

"Hey, Haze, how's it going?" Shane asked, untangling himself, careful not to drop his sandwich. Justin nodded at her and hung back.

Hazel and Shane had dated off and on, and Justin was never sure if they were on or off. She was clingy, and Justin always teased him about her being his stalker. But tonight, Shane seemed out of it, neither happy nor annoyed by Hazel.

"I'm just so glad to see you, I mean I hardly know anyone here!" she slurred, leaning a little too heavily on him.

"Aww, I'm sorry. I was just going to chat with Justin a bit. Can I catch up with you in a little while?"

"Oh. Um, okay, I guess so. I'll see you later then." Despite the smile, she wasn't able to hide her disappointment. Justin looked away, feeling bad for her.

"That would be awesome. Can't wait to hang out," Shane offered. Hazel beamed and nodded before heading off to the kitchen.

"Dude, she's everywhere we go," Justin said.

"I know you don't get it. I mean, I told you before, Hazel had a rough childhood. I'm all she's got."

"Yeah, I know, you said that. But maybe she needs therapy or something."

"Naw, she'll be good once she's out on her own."

They found a quiet corner in the living room to hang out. Justin looked around at the small groups of seniors, thankful they managed to find an empty spot.

"So what's been going on? Haven't seen you around much this last week," Justin said. Shane stared off into space and Justin snapped his fingers in front of him.

"Yeah, sorry dude. My sister was home this week so there were a lot of family dinners. You know how my parents get when Sloane's home. We have to all be together and hear about all the amazing shit she's doing at school. Just, same old shit." Shane's head dropped to his chest, lost in his own thoughts.

Wow, didn't expect that question to be such a buzzkill.

Justin didn't know what to say, his mind stumbling over the right response to try to get them back to the party and having a good time.

"You okay?" was what he finally settled on. *Prolific*. He kicked himself.

"Yeah, I'm just feeling dark. I hate to ask again, but I need something else, man. What do you have?" Shane asked, glancing around the room.

Justin hesitated. He didn't want to refuse his best friend, but he also felt like Shane had been asking a little too frequently. "I definitely have something that can take the edge off," Justin said, digging in his pocket. "But listen, you can't drink when you take them. I don't know if this party is the best place to try 'em for the first time."

"I wasn't really planning on drinking anyway."

Justin's hand stilled in his pocket, the small pill bottle clutched between his fingers. Maybe he could distract Shane, get him to forget about the pills.

"So, your sister's here? I didn't know she was back from school." Justin barely knew anything about Shane's sister other than she went to some sort of boarding school. They'd met once in passing when she was home for winter break last year.

"Apparently one of the football players that lives next door to us goes running with her in the morning when she's home. I didn't know." Shane didn't seem to know or care about any more details.

"Oh, and she's meeting up with him here? Who is it?" Justin cringed, thinking about the guys in the other room.

"Oliver. He's not too bad."

"Ah, yeah he's not the worst, at least." Justin laughed

then sighed at Shane's impatient expression when his eyes dropped to Justin's pocket.

Giving pills to his friends had never been part of his plan—not that he'd ever had a plan. Making easy money off one of the douchebag athletes? Sure, he didn't mind doing that. But Shane, being Shane, had started out by simply being curious.

"Just let me try one. I mean, you're selling them. You might as well know how they make someone feel," Shane had argued.

Justin had reluctantly agreed Shane had a point. He hadn't been interested in trying them himself—he hated any kind of medicine or substance that altered the way he thought or felt. The thought alone made him panicky. But he had been asked before what the pills made him feel like. He'd made something up on the spot, but now that he was sitting here with Shane, he wondered if it wasn't such a bad idea.

"Fine, one. Just one, dude." Justin had pulled the small bag from his backpack and took out one of the pills. Grinning wide, Shane had held his hand out. Shane's excitement had made Justin pause but before he could change his mind, Shane had snatched the pill and popped it in his mouth.

That had been the first time, but Shane had liked it so much that he continued to ask whenever they hung out. Sometimes, Justin lied and said he was out. He never sold it to his best friend, but when Shane offered to buy them, Justin refused. Mostly because he didn't want to make a close friend a customer. Then it became personal. The other kids who bought from him only approached when they wanted a little something extra to party with. Shane had reached a point where he was using them to cope with daily problems.

Justin tried not to think about it; he wanted to enjoy the party. But he was worried about Shane.

"Okay, fine. But seriously, dude, promise me, you *won't* drink. Listen, I only do this because I need the money to save up for college, I'm not trying to make my friends rely on it. I don't know about you driving home either. Come find me if you're sleepy or *anything*, okay?" Justin knew he was crossing a line, which was all the more reason to protect his best friend from doing anything stupid.

"Sure, dude, no problem!" Shane's mood turned drastically upbeat. Justin opened a small bottle and discretely slipped the yellow and green capsule into Shane's waiting hand. Shane immediately swallowed it with a gulp of his soda.

"What are you guys doing over here? Sulking?" Chelsea asked as she walked by with one of the football players leading her to the stairs.

"Just hanging out. You good?" Justin asked, nodding his chin at Jordan.

"Hell yeah," Chelsea giggled and turned back to Jordan, nuzzling his chest.

Justin rolled his eyes as they went upstairs.

"I'm still hungry," Justin complained, swinging his attention back to Shane.

"Dude, I feel kind of funny. What exactly was that pill anyway?' Shane asked as they headed back to the kitchen.

17

GAME NIGHT

"So this is what we have to choose from," Justin said, gesturing at the stack of games. "I should have gotten some new ones, but I didn't really think about it. Sorry."

"I think we can make do," Hannah assuaged, smiling at him. She didn't know what the others were thinking, but she wanted them to be interested in the games he'd set out and hoped no one complained.

"Well, anyway… congrats on your engagement, Nick! I saw the announcement in the paper last week." Justin leaned forward on his knees, his gangly legs awkwardly propped up.

"Oh yeah. Thanks, man." Nick nodded but quickly averted his eyes.

With Justin's attempt to steer the conversation falling

flat, Hannah looked away, embarrassed, and fiddled with a loose string on her pant leg.

"So? Who is she, man? How long have you been dating? Give us the scoop."

Hannah jumped at Alex's thunderous voice. She'd already lost count of how many drinks he'd had, but given how everyone's demeanor shifted, they were in for a long night.

"Her name is Alicia Goldberg. We started dating about a year ago."

Hannah leaned forward, her interest piqued. "How'd you meet?" Even though she wanted to come across as Justin's caring girlfriend, she was truly curious about Nick's relationship. Alicia Goldberg was a wealthy and connected socialite and seemed like such an odd match for him.

"Ahh, through my boss, actually. He's her father. She came to a fundraiser we hosted last year. He introduced us."

Nick refused to make eye contact with her, and Hannah faltered for a second, not sure what to say next. *Why was he being so weird about it?*

"Wait. Alicia Goldberg, Ralph Goldberg's daughter? Ralph Goldberg of Goldberg and Goldberg Associates?" Lucy blurted, suddenly fascinated.

"Yep, one and the same."

Nick seemed reluctant to divulge any more information. *Curious*, Hannah pondered.

"Remember that girl Nick dated in ninth grade before Lauren? I think her name was Deidre? Dog-*o*." Alex gagged before doubling over in a fit of hysterics.

"Deidre wasn't that bad. She just had a *five*head," Lucy deadpanned, causing everyone to burst into laughter.

Hannah looked around at the group, laughing at jokes about people she didn't know, sharing memories she didn't have. She hadn't expected to feel like such an outsider. Knowing they hadn't seen each other in years had given her false hope that they were basically strangers too. But alcohol was lubricating their social interactions, putting them at ease.

She glanced down at her full glass. Her propriety wouldn't allow her to get drunk and sloppy. She didn't even *like* to drink.

Reluctantly, she forced herself to take a gulp, if for no other reason than to stop feeling like she didn't fit in.

"Well, it's not all about looks. Some of us have more to offer than just a pretty face and an empty head." Lauren dipped her head towards Alex, and they all laughed again. Hannah forced a smile.

"Let's play this game," Lucy interrupted from the other side of the room. "It's a team game, so we can just split into two teams." She held up one of the boxes and waved it around.

"Perfect! This game is hysterical!" Justin jumped out of his chair.

He pulled the coffee table towards the center of the group while Lucy brought the box over. She handed it to Justin who set up the board and shuffled the cards. The premise of the game was to guess what your teammate was saying from a bunch of gibberish on the card. It seemed like a good choice to keep things lighthearted.

Most of their drinks disappeared quickly, evidence of their shared anxiety. As the game progressed and voices grew louder, they each trickled in and out of the kitchen, refilling their drinks.

The dim light of the living room flickered, casting ominous shadows across the walls. Against the backdrop of laughter and clinking glasses, Hannah bustled around the table, scooping up empty plates and setting up new rounds of cards for the game.

The evening had been relatively tame so far—playful teasing, funny moments—but there was an undercurrent that threatened to shatter at any moment. Hannah played the wallflower well, watching Justin and his friends share a knowing glance when they thought she wasn't looking. Their voices were a little too stiff, their smiles a little too wide.

"Alright, everyone ready for round two?" Justin asked.

A red-faced Alex sat up straighter on the couch. He'd hardly contributed to the game. "Are we just going to ignore the elephant in the room?" he asked.

Everyone went silent and looked at him. Hannah clasped her lips shut, hoping they would forget she was in the room, but she couldn't help but notice the others' reactions.

Nick and Justin glared, shooting daggers with their eyes, clearly trying to send a meaningful look to signal Alex to shut up.

"Alex, not now," Lauren hissed, grabbing his arm, her eyes darting nervously towards Hannah. Hannah didn't miss a beat.

"What elephant?" Hannah asked. She looked around at everyone.

The air stilled. No one breathed. But then there was a sudden burst of laughter from Nick. "Nothing, nothing! He's just teasing."

Hannah blew out a slow breath. The room tingled with energy, but it wasn't excitement or revelry. A heaviness that hadn't been there moments before settled over them like a descending fog. She might be the outsider, but she could feel the weight of it.

"Oh yeah, you know, just stupid stuff from way back. Nothing important." Lucy waved her hand around.

Alex, who'd been staring at his drink, cleared his throat. "Fine, round two—let's do this." His hand gripped his drink a little too tightly while his eyes narrowed on Justin and the others.

Hannah sensed the tension growing around her. Tight smiles, darting glances, nervous shifting. She wanted them to explain. But how much could she push?

"I'm guessing it's something more than just stupid stuff from way back. Tell me all your dark teenage secrets!" A mischievous smirk tugged her lips upward as she feigned innocence. Leaning back, she waited.

"Oh, it's nothing, babe," Justin intervened, his smile not reaching his eyes. "Just old memories, you know how it is."

But Alex's glare was still fixed on the group, his mouth set in a tight line. Would he say more? Hannah silently willed his drunk tongue to loosen up.

"Yeah, memories," Nick said quickly, standing up and crossing the room to change the music. "Let's get back to the game, huh?"

Hannah pushed down the feeling of annoyance, as she debated pressing them for more, but they'd all closed up like clams. She pursed her lips and stared down at her hands in her lap. *Fine, let them keep their secrets.*

The silence lingered before Justin forced another laugh. "Alright, alright, no more cryptic talk. Let's have fun. Just play, yeah?"

But the energy had shifted. They were all playing the game, but the stakes had changed.

It wasn't about the cards anymore.

It was about the secret they were desperate to bury.

18

SENIOR PARTY

By midnight, the party had broken off into small groups as the number of discarded cups scattered about the sticky kitchen island had increased.

Sitting on barstools at a small section of the counter they'd cleaned off, Justin and Shane played a card game.

Lauren sat beside them, swinging her legs back and forth. "You guys... I'm so bored," she whined, proof she'd had much more to drink than usual. "Are you going to play that game *all* night?"

Justin laughed off her grumbling.

"Where is everyone, anyway?" she asked.

"Alex is out on the patio. Can't you hear him?" Justin answered, gesturing towards the open glass doors. Alex's voice echoed through the house, followed by his obnoxious donkey laugh that always got worse the more he drank.

"Oh yeah. Maybe Lucy's out there!" Lauren said, hopping down from the counter and losing her balance.

On instinct, Justin reached out and caught her. "You good?" he asked. "Maybe you should eat something else." He pointed to the island where the food had been picked over. Lauren agreed and grabbed a handful of crackers.

"Okay, I'm okay. Had more than I thought, but I'm okay," she slurred before heading out onto the patio with Alex.

Shane and Justin returned to their game, engrossed in a debate about one of their favorite old school horror movies, when a girl's voice interrupted them.

"Hey, Shane."

"Hey, sis," Shane responded, smiling wider than usual.

Justin followed his gaze until his eyes landed on a round-faced girl standing by the kitchen sink. She looked familiar. She stared back, the smile falling from her face the moment she saw Justin.

Justin's stomach dropped. Something was off, he just didn't know what.

"Justin, you remember my sister, Sloane, right? I think y'all met over winter break."

"Oh right." Justin's voice was faint, confused. Thinking back, he remembered running into her at their house when she was home from boarding school, but something was still bugging him.

When Shane was around his sister, he seemed more normal, like the dark cloud that usually hung over him was lifted. He was a different Shane, but Justin couldn't quite put his finger on why.

"Hey, babe, there you are!" Oliver, the football player she'd come with, burst in and made a beeline for Sloane. He scooped her up under his beefy arm and left.

Hazel rushed into the kitchen from the patio just as Oliver was leaving with Shane's sister. She grinned as soon as she saw Shane.

"Let's do shots!" She grabbed a bottle from the counter and reached for the stack of disposable shot glasses, but there were only a few left. Most of them were discarded throughout the kitchen or piled up in the sink. Few had made it to the trash can.

"Oh, we're good." Shane waved a hand.

"Come on! We never get to party together!" she insisted.

Shane shook his head no again, his eyes darting nervously to Justin, who also shook his head.

"Nah, I'm driving," Justin said when she turned her pleading eyes on him.

"Yeah, me too. And how do *you* plan on getting home tonight, Haze?" Shane teased.

Hazel pouted. "Come *on*. One shot won't hurt. We won't be leaving for hours. Besides, Chelsea said anyone could crash here that needed to. There are tons of places to sleep."

Time slowed as Justin watched Shane change his mind.

It was just one shot, Justin said to himself. *How bad could it be?*

For a while Justin zoned out, scrolling on his phone,

looking at pictures other seniors had already uploaded online. Without thinking, he got up and grabbed a coke from the fridge. He sat back down, leaving Shane and Hazel to their flirtatious banter. When he finally snapped out of it, he realized at least thirty minutes had passed.

"Okay, one more!" Hazel squealed, jumping up and down, pouring them each another shot. "Cheers!" she said as they threw it back.

"There you are, Hazel! You *have* to come see this!" The girl's voice ricocheted around the empty kitchen.

"Okay, okay. I'm gonna go hang. I'll see you later?" Hazel asked, leaning over Shane. He turned and let her slobber all over him, but he barely returned the kiss. A look of disappointment crossed her face, but she just backed away and jogged after her friend.

"Have fun!" Shane called, his words slurring together.

Lost in thought, Justin stared after the girls, still trying to figure out where he knew Shane's sister from. When it hit him, his stomach plummeted.

"I feel sick," Justin said and ran to the kitchen sink, retching.

"Dude, you didn't even drink anything." The pitch of Shane's voice was off, his words garbling together like he'd been drinking all night long.

Justin rinsed his mouth under the faucet and turned around, shaken by the unrecognizable tone of his best friend. "You okay?" Justin asked.

Shane shook his head, distraught. "It's just—my life is shit, man. My sister's just so perfect, right? I'm such a loser. My parent's fucking hate me," Shane muttered, his words hanging thick in the air.

Justin's head fell. This wasn't his first time hearing Shane say these things.

Shane slumped over the countertop, his eyes distant.

Tonight was different—it was clear he believed what he was saying. He droned on, listing the reasons he was a loser, his voice trailing off.

"Dude, you're not a loser," Justin said, trying to steady his voice despite the tightness in his chest.

He had seen Shane spiral in this dark trance before. It was always scary, but this… It had the hair on his arms standing at attention. His muscles went taut, and the air buzzed with a different sort of energy.

Shane let out a hollow laugh. "Oh yeah? I can't even do one thing right. She has it all together. I'm just... nothing."

The words were raw, each one a sharp stab to Justin's gut. He hated hearing Shane talk this way. It made his bowels turn liquid. Shane had been struggling for so long, but he was sinking faster. Justin thought about the pills— the ones Shane had been using to dull the pain. He'd tried to cut Shane off, but the weight of everything must have been too much for Shane to bear.

Tonight, with the alcohol, Shane was in dangerous territory.

Justin's heart raced as Shane's face clouded over with bitterness. The mix of alcohol and pills made Shane unpredictable, and Justin knew how dark things could get when he was like this—too dark. Too far gone.

"Shane…" Justin said carefully, stepping closer, his voice shaking. "It's not you. It's the way they treat you, the way they compare you to her. But you're not a loser. You're *not*. Do you hear me?"

Shane stared at the counter, his eyes blank. When he finally spoke, his voice was flat, unemotional. Detached.

"It's hard to just... be. I'm worthless, and nothing is ever gonna change that. It'd be easier if I would–"

"If you would, what, Shane?"

Shane's cold gaze met Justin's. "Fade away."

A surge of panic rose in Justin's chest, his heart beat in his throat. He could see it happening—the breakdown. The spiral with a tragic ending. He sensed, deep in his gut, that Shane wasn't just venting or moaning about life being unfair—he was sinking into something far worse. He needed help. Professional help.

Lost in a haze, Shane barely moved. He lowered his eyes, but they didn't focus on anything. Eventually, he stood up, unsteady, and started towards the door, his steps slow and unsure.

A dark realization hit Justin like a train.

Shane was about to do something stupid—something that would make this all worse.

Justin chased after him.

"Shane! Wait!"

He had to stop him. But Shane didn't acknowledge Justin, didn't even slow down. He was too far gone, too deep in his head. Bile rose in Justin's throat. He couldn't let him go, not like this. Shane was not in his right mind. If Justin didn't get through to him–*now*–he was going to do something he would regret.

"Please, just stop!" Justin pleaded, grabbing Shane's arm. "Don't do this, man."

Shane jerked out of Justin's grasp. "You don't get it. No one gets it."

Justin's pulse raced. He reached for Shane again. "I get it. But we're in this together. You're not a loser."

Justin's heart pounded in his ears so loud he could barely hear himself think. Panicked, he debated what else he could say or do.

Should I find Sloane? Justin wondered, looking around for a glimpse of her. *She always brings out the best in him...*

19

TWO WEEKS BEFORE
SENIOR PARTY

Lucy threw her math textbook into her locker and slammed the door with a lot more force than needed. Her latest test grade had soured her mood, and she was kicking herself for declining Nick's offer to help her study again. *I'll never pass now, without his help.*

"What'd that locker ever do to you?"

Alex's voice broke her out of her thoughts. He was only teasing, she knew, but the usual zing of annoyance at him flowed through her like an electric current.

She whirled around and blew air out of her mouth, causing her bangs to flutter across her forehead. She leaned back against the lockers, and shrugged.

"I got a 70 on my math test."

"Hey, at least you passed!" Noting her reaction, he was quick to add, "Did you ask Nick to help you study? I'm sure he wouldn't mind."

"No." Lucy sighed, shouldering her way around Alex as she slung her backpack over one shoulder. "I'm going to grab lunch."

Alex pushed his way into the crowd to keep up with her. "Let's ask him now."

Alex took her by the elbow and guided her around the corner into a classroom. The room was full of students who worked on the school paper during their lunch period. They glanced up, but their focus immediately went back to their computers. Except for Nick.

"Hey, what's up?" he asked, his eyes darting between Alex and Lucy.

Lucy pulled her arm away, not wanting to feel like a kid whose parent was dragging her to a tutor. She ushered Alex back to the door. "I'll catch up with you later, okay?"

Alex didn't hesitate. He leaned in to kiss her, and she swerved out of reach, not hiding her disgust. Unfazed, Alex darted down the hall.

Odd. Usually he was a pushier. *Probably didn't want to look bad in front of his best friend.*

Lucy faced the room but avoided looking directly at Nick. "I need help in math again. Alex wanted me to ask you."

"Yeah, I can help you with that." One of the other students coughed, and Nick's voice dropped to a whisper. "I wanted to talk to you anyway."

He glanced around and made eye contact with a girl who was watching them over her computer. She ducked down behind the screen when Nick saw her.

"Let's go next door."

Nick directed her into the printing room. Most students weren't allowed access but as the newspaper editor, Nick had free rein.

"Listen, Alex has been my best friend since forever," Nick began, his voice uncertain. He shifted from foot to foot, glancing down at his hands before meeting Lucy's eyes. "But we're... we're really very different people."

Lucy's expression tightened. Her lips pressed into a thin line, and her shoulders sagged. She was caught between regret, resignation, and a lingering emotion she couldn't name.

With a sharp inhale, she spoke the words that could alter the course of everything.

"I know where you're going with this, Nick. But—" She hesitated, the bitter taste of the words choking her. "You know, what you're hinting at? That could never happen."

She shook her head, but the movement was more to convince herself than him.

"Everyone would hate us. We'd lose our best friends. We'd ruin the rest of our senior year." Her voice faltered, her breath catching as the weight settled over her. She tried to steady herself, feeling ridiculous. Ultimately, despite her intense attraction to Nick, she knew Nick wasn't who she longed to be with. He was simply a distraction from what she really wanted.

Nick's jaw clenched, his fingers twisting together. "Being with someone you don't want to be with is wrong," he muttered, the words rough. His gaze dropped to the floor for a moment, then snapped back to her, as though looking away was too difficult.

Lucy raised an eyebrow, as she crossed her arms. "Did you really think I was going to dump Alex and jump into something with you?" The words hung heavy in the air between them. "That's not how it works. There's no future for us, Nick."

For a moment, silence lingered between them. Nick lowered his voice to an urgent whisper. "Yeah, I mean, I wouldn't expect us to go public or anything, but I could at least be with you without feeling like I'm betraying Alex. Without that guilt."

Something akin to vulnerability crossed his face.

Did I miss that before? The air between them was alive in a way that made her dizzy. As much as she wanted to be mad at him, she couldn't ignore the way her senses heightened around him. The heat from his body caused a shiver to run down her back, the hairs on her neck to dance.

An ache to reach out and touch him overwhelmed her, and her body betrayed her.

She edged closer. Her leg brushed against his, and their eyes locked. Nick's gaze dropped to her lips. A low moan escaped his throat, and they inched even closer.

"It's so hard not to kiss you right now."

The low rumble of Nick's voice feathered through her whole body. She leaned in, desperate for their lips to meet, and begged the universe to forgive this one indiscretion.

"Hey Nick, can you look at this rough draft for me?"

At Hazel's interruption, they both sprang upright and away from each other.

Hazel's face was a complete blank, clueless as to what she'd walked in on.

Lucy muttered an excuse and squeezed past Hazel.

"Is she okay?" Lucy heard Hazel ask as she sprinted down the hall.

20

GAME NIGHT

The games were starting to get a little more competitive and not in the playful way they had been. Seemingly lost in their own memories, the underlying tension bubbled up and simmered.

Justin's palms were sweaty again, and the comfortable relaxation the drinks had provided was slipping away. He needed a moment to gather his thoughts and pull himself together. He got up and offered to refill everyone's drinks.

"I'll grab some more snacks too," he said, fumbling with the tray of empty glasses and plates.

"Let me help you," Hannah offered, jumping up and gathering the rest of the plates.

Justin wanted to protest, needing a moment alone in the kitchen, but his throat felt tight, and he couldn't summon the words. The evening was moving along as he'd expected, but he couldn't shake the nerves that were building. He knew everything would come to a head soon, and he wanted to be in full control. He was annoyed with himself for not having found a way to have this reunion without Hannah. He wanted to bring up what had happened but not in front of her. He was beginning to realize that she was going to make what he needed to do tonight so much harder. *What was I thinking? Having her here is such a risk.*

In the kitchen, he gulped down a glass of cold water as Hannah made up another small platter of snacks. He felt her watching him, and he finally turned to her. She looked like she was ready to pounce.

Immediately, she began questioning him. "What was everyone hinting at in there? What happened? You guys seem so tense about it." Hannah leveled him with a stare, her questions sounding more like an interrogation than casual curiosity. He wondered if she could sense that it was something so much bigger than 'stupid teenage stuff.'

"You know, just high school drama. Nothing worth rehashing." Justin's voice betrayed him, cracking mid-sentence. He chastised himself. He needed to pull it together. Deep regret gnawed at him; he should have had them over when she was out of town or busy with one of her late night work events.

"You must think I'm extremely naive. Just tell me!" Hannah demanded, her annoyance evident.

He stifled a jump, his mind racing, trying to think of something he could tell her that would satisfy her. "Just, you know, Lucy and Alex dated in high school," he started, his voice a low whisper, not wanting their guests to over-hear him.

"Right…" she said, drawing out the word while looking skeptical.

"Lucy cheated on Alex with Nick. As in… Alex's best friend. Everyone found out one night, and it led to a big fight." Justin shrugged, refusing to make eye contact. "We haven't hung out since."

Hannah stood perfectly still. Justin's eyes darted to her and found her staring at him, eyes narrowed.

"That's it? That's all that happened?"

Justin's stomach dropped. He couldn't quite figure out what she was thinking, but her tone was cold, suggesting something beyond annoyance.

"Yeah," he said, half laughing. "I told you it was stupid. We were kids, so it seemed like a big deal back then." Even Justin realized how inadequate his explanation was. It didn't explain why everyone was being so weird about it now. If it had only been teenage relationship drama, surely they'd be laughing it off.

"Justin, there's something else, I can tell." She grabbed his arm, keeping him from heading back into the room with the others. Her voice was clipped, almost angry, and her nails dug into his skin. He flinched, pulling away. She quickly released her grip and rearranged her face.

"Sorry," she said, glancing at the marks on his arm. "But you know you can tell me anything."

He released a heavy sigh. "Yeah, I know. You've been great, Hannah." He paused, setting the tray back on the counter. He gathered her in his arms and kissed her. She leaned into it, her tongue darting between his teeth, and he groaned, pushing her back against the counter.

This, he thought, *this is how she gets me every time*. No other girl had ever made him crave them more. She was usually aloof, almost a bit of an ice princess the rest of the time. But when it came to their physical connection, she was a tigress, devouring him in a way that made it hard for him to think about anything else.

"I wish you'd tell me. It's clearly bothering you," she whispered against his neck, trailing her nails softly down his back and looping one leg over his hip. He gripped her thigh, the faux leather giving him a thrill as he thought about peeling those pants off of her.

"It's just… it's a lot, Hannah." He let out a shaky breath, and she moved her hips against him, grinding against his growing erection. The way she could bring him to this state so quickly made him feel like a teenager all over again. His resolve began to crumble.

He pressed his face into the curve of her neck, struggling to keep his composure. His breath came in shallow, desperate gasps, the weight of everything pressing down on him all at once. The closeness of her should have been a comfort, but all he felt was the sting of memories, too sharp and too raw.

"It was horrible." His voice was raspy and thick with pain.

She froze against him, breaking the spell. "What was?"

He pulled back, realizing he was about to tell her everything. "I… I… I'll tell you everything later, okay? After everyone leaves," he said, dropping his head to his chest and taking a deep inhale to steady himself. He waited until the blood rushed back to his brain so he could think clearly.

Hannah let out a huff of frustration, but she didn't

pursue it further. Scooping up the tray of drinks, she breezed past him. "I'll bring these in," she said, leaving him leaning against the counter as his erection wilted.

21

SENIOR PARTY

Lauren came storming through the kitchen, her shoes heavy against the tiles as she slammed into Justin's shoulder. "I still can't find Lucy," she snapped at him, her face flushed, her eyes darting around the room in a panic.

"Haven't seen her, but I have bigger problems. Sorry L, I gotta go find where Shane went." Justin tried to maneuver around Lauren, pushing past her with a sense of urgency.

"Why, what's going on?" Lauren asked, her voice laced with ever more confusion and concern.

"I'll tell you later." Justin's whole body went rigid with anxiety. He turned away from Lauren.

"Lucy and Shane can't both be missing." Lauren's face crumbled, and she looked like she was about to cry.

Justin paused, swallowing an irritated sigh. Whatever was up with Shane wasn't Lauren's fault. She had been looking for Lucy for too long now, and he knew she was worried about her friend. But right now, he had to catch up with Shane and keep him from doing something crazy.

"I'm sure Lucy is around somewhere. Did you check upstairs?"

"Earlier, but maybe I should check again." Unsure, Lauren's voice faded away.

"I think you should. You go do that, and I'm going to go find Shane," Justin said, already moving on. He gave Lauren's arm a quick squeeze and then ducked around her to head outside before she could protest. His heart pounded, realizing he'd lost precious time talking to Lauren. What if Shane had disappeared into the night?

Out on the patio, he quickly scanned the crowd, trying to find Shane's lanky, distinctive figure in the crowd. *Too many people.* Justin's shoulders slumped. Waves of panic washed over him, his body hot and his hands tingling. He forced himself to calm down and think straight.

He studied the pool where some kids were splashing around. He bet they'd been too preoccupied to have noticed Shane. They didn't even seem to notice Justin. His eyes darted to the perimeter of the property, where cars had parked on the lawn wrapping around the house.

Finally, his gaze landed on Shane who was walking past the cars at a clipped pace despite not being able to walk in a straight line.

Justin took off after him, suddenly glad he hadn't been drinking.

Something in the night air hummed with danger. His gut told him.

Chelsea's house sat high up on a long, winding road, secluded from the rest of town. Not too far down, where the road hooked around a perilous curve, was a cliff. Memories of Shane joking about throwing himself off that cliff ricochetted around Justin's mind. So many cars had gotten into accidents there, careening through the guardrail and sailing over the edge.

Justin picked up his pace as he closed in on Shane.

"Bro, wait up!" he shouted, breathing heavily. He reached out and grabbed Shane's shoulder, but Shane shrugged him off.

"Man, just go back to the party. I'm fine." Each word came out in a slurred huff of breath.

Justin tried to steady the nerves in his stomach and clear his panicked thoughts. "Just let me talk to you for a minute!" Desperation hovered over him like a rain cloud. His throat tightened, and he forced himself to focus on breathing normally.

"Nothing you say changes anything!" Shane said. Anger vibrated off him, but at least he'd stopped.

Justin used the chance to think of what to do next. He clenched and unclenched his fists, willing the tingling to go away. They stared at each other in silence. The moment lingered too long. Justin's body stiffened, almost as if it knew before he did… Finally, Justin realized he'd lost the opportunity to bring Shane back from the brink.

Shane puffed out an annoyed sigh and turned around, continuing his brisk stride away from the house.

22

GAME NIGHT

auren leaned back on Justin's couch, dwelling on how uneasy the night was becoming. She wondered how Rich was doing with Cody's bedtime. Glancing around, she watched Alex at the other corner of the couch slurp down his drink, sandwich clutched in his other hand.

Shaking her head to herself, she turned to examine Nick sitting in one of the chairs angled away from her. He flipped through some book he'd found on one of the shelves. She couldn't see what he was looking at, but he was deeply enthralled with whatever it was.

Turning her attention to Lucy, who was standing with her back to Lauren as she perused the long wall of books, knickknacks and games, Lauren's heart rate sped up. Lucy was still remarkably beautiful, not a hair out of place, her outfit immaculate. But she was so thin. *Is she sick? If so, is it serious?* Her body was all sharp angles now, her bones protruding beneath her clothes. With a sallow complexion and sunken cheeks, her eyes appeared bigger, yet more forlorn than ever. Gone were the curves that had matched her sassy and bubbly personality in high school.

Lucy turned and caught Lauren watching her. Lucy smiled and glanced over at Nick. In the next heartbeat, horror flashed across her face.

"Is that our yearbook?" she asked, her voice shrill. She moved closer and peered over Nick's shoulder.

Alex snapped out of his stupor and scooted closer to Nick. "Really? Let's see then."

Nick set the book on the coffee table. The three of them leaned forward and began commenting on the photos.

Lauren sat up straighter, curious about the yearbook too. Of course she had her own copy, but she'd stuffed it in a box that was packed away somewhere in the attic. She'd never wanted to flip through it again.

"Hey, did you guys hear about Coach Troy?" Alex asked. The others nodded. Of course they'd heard; it had been all over the news.

"Yeah, dude, but Coach Troy was Justin's stepdad, so maybe we shouldn't talk about that," Nick hissed, glancing towards the kitchen.

Lucy's eyes grew wide. "Oh right!"

"Well, they were divorced when it happened," Alex said, taking a bite of his sandwich. "I ran into him once, with some chick he was dating. She looked like she was barely over eighteen."

Lucy's cringed, disgust outlining her features, and then

gagged. Jabbing her finger at one of the pictures, she said, "Hey, look at this!" Alex and Justin leaned closer and laughed, the three of them talking at once.

While everyone was preoccupied, Lauren slipped into the entryway where the basket of phones was sitting. Digging around for hers, she pulled it out and immediately noticed a missed message from Rich. She wondered why they hadn't heard it ringing. She checked the volume and realized the phone had been silenced.

Her eyebrows furrowed as she glanced around behind her, wondering what had happened. She remembered turning the volume up as loud as it would go. She couldn't have accidentally hit the silence switch, could she?

Her mind felt foggy. Even though she'd only had one cocktail, it was a lot stronger than she was accustomed to. The others' voices as they laughed and reminisced over the photos in the yearbook made it hard for her to focus. *Think.* She tried to remember if she had silenced it before dropping it in the basket.

Glancing over her shoulder, she quickly read and responded to Rich's message. Thankfully, he'd only sent a photo of Cody, fast asleep, with a simple message. *"We're good here. Have fun."* She breathed a sigh of relief that it had been an easy bedtime for him.

She responded to a couple of other messages and sent a quick email. Hearing Hannah coming back from the kitchen, she tossed her phone in the basket and darted back to join the others. She stood to the side of the coffee table and noticed the yearbook flipped open to the section of various student clubs. Kids posing with the school newspaper, Chess Club and Art Club, all grinning, trapped in time.

"Where did you find that?" Hannah asked as she set a tray of drinks down on the coffee table. Oddly enough, she sounded annoyed, almost angry.

Nick cleared his throat and started to answer just as Justin came in with a tray of snacks.

"Oh, I'd pulled that out. For old times sake," Justin said. Despite the casual tone, his face flushed from the neck up.

Something nagged at Lauren. Why would that have been such an absurd idea? They were childhood friends who hadn't seen one another since high school...

"There's Lauren!" Lucy said, lunging forward and pointing to the photo of Art Club where Lauren sat grinning ear to ear, front and center, sprawled out like she'd just ended a dance routine.

"Who's that?" Hannah asked, her finger tapping on a boy standing off by himself in the back of the Art Club. The others froze, eyes flicking between one another frantically.

After a long pause, Justin answered. "That's Shane. He was my best friend in high school."

"Oh, you didn't keep in touch? Where is he? Why didn't you invite him?" Hannah straightened, turning to Justin.

The mood instantly darkened, the tension becoming palpable. Lauren's heart thudded in her ears, spots danced in her vision. Lucy audibly swallowed. Alex paled and slumped back down on the sofa.

Justin stared at Hannah, unblinking, looking as though he was trying to calm his voice before answering.

Glancing up, it was Nick who answered. "Shane died at the end of senior year."

"Oh my gosh!" Hannah clasped a hand over her mouth,

her reaction overtly melodramatic. "I'm so sorry! What happened?"

Lauren's face contorted uncontrollably. How tacky of Hannah to dig for details. Irritation at Hannah began eating at Lauren. On the one hand, Hannah was Justin's girlfriend, and Lauren could understand her reasons for wanting to know all of this. But on the other hand, it reeked of suspicious vulgarity to press for details when they were all clearly uncomfortable.

Justin swallowed hard. "He was hit by a car." He stopped and took a deep breath. "Well, he'd been drinking, and they thought maybe he'd... stepped out in front of the car on purpose."

"That poor driver! Did they go to jail?" Hannah asked, her eyes saucers, but her voice was syrupy sweet.

A blanket of tension fell over the room, and everyone shifted awkwardly.

"um... no, it was a hit and run." Nick stood up, suddenly taking control over the situation. "But, you know, this is probably not the time to talk about all this. Maybe we should just play another game?"

Justin glanced at him, a flash of gratitude crossing his face as he sank back into his recliner.

Lauren stood frozen, her eyes darting around at the others. She fought a wave of nausea as a memory flooded over her. She swallowed hard, forcing the lump down. On edge, she watched Alex filter through multiple emotions, and silently pleaded with him not to say anything. As drunk as he was, anything he said or did was completely unpredictable.

"Right! What game should we play next?" Lucy's voice

broke the tension, but her forced cheerfulness fooled no one.

Hannah narrowed her eyes, her lips puckering, but she said nothing.

"Good idea," Lauren agreed.

The two went over to the table with the small stack of board games, both of them trying to gloss over the obvious turmoil.

23

SENIOR PARTY

Lauren stumbled up the stairs of Chelsea's house, her shoes clomping unsteadily against the intricate marble steps. The party downstairs was in full swing, but Lauren was done with the noise and chaos of the crowd. She had come to this party with one purpose: to hang out with Lucy. After all, they had planned to celebrate the end of senior year together. But after over an hour of aimless mingling and watching her friend disappear into the throng of people, Lauren was fed up. She had no interest in hanging around by herself any longer.

She passed open doors along the hallway, peering inside each one with growing frustration. The dim light from the rooms illuminated only bits of the house—walls decorated with expensive art, expensive furniture, and the occasional half-empty bottle of liquor left behind. But there was no sign of Lucy anywhere.

After checking all the open rooms, her patience finally reached its limit. With a quiet sigh, she tossed her hair back and decided to check behind closed doors. She marched towards the closest one, hesitation causing her footsteps to falter. But at this point, she didn't care anymore. She shoved the doubt aside. She needed to find her friend.

"Fuck it," she mumbled to herself, swinging the door open.

"What the hell?" the guy said. Lauren couldn't remember the football player's name. He shot upright on the bed, and Lauren froze, her heart skipping a beat. She blinked, trying to focus on what was happening in front of her. The guy was kneeling on the bed, and Chelsea was lying back beneath him, her upper body exposed, a wicked smile on her face.

"Shit, sorry," Lauren apologized, her face flushing crimson with embarrassment. She instinctively took a step back, ready to bolt, but Chelsea just laughed and waved her off. Lauren yanked the door shut and leaned against it.

She had to be quicker. Reaching for the next door, she opened it and peered in. Just a couple seniors passed out on the bed.

Suddenly, she heard Lucy's bubbly laughter followed by a squeal. Lauren turned towards the sound coming from across the hall. She reached for the handle and let the door fall open. Too drunk to have thought about what she might be walking into, her mouth fell open in shock.

Lucy, entirely naked, straddling Nick on the bed. Nick's eyes were closed, his head tipped back.

"Lucy?" Lauren breathed, but they didn't seem to hear.

Boiling heat washed over Lauren's body, flushing her face and traveling down her neck. Her heart dropped to her stomach, not wanting to believe what she was seeing. The room spun, and she struggled to catch her breath.

She could feel a panic attack coming on, but she squeezed her eyes shut, inhaling deeply through her nose. *Maybe I imagined it. Maybe it's not really her.* Lauren opened her eyes again when Lucy said something to Nick. He grunted in response, his hands grasping at her hips.

Anger and something that felt remarkably close to jealousy built within Lauren. The onslaught of emotions broke free, and she snapped.

"What the fuck, Lucy?"

The couple jerked apart.

"Oh shit," Nick said, fumbling for the sheets to cover himself while reaching for his pants on the floor. As he shimmied into his clothes, Lucy stumbled around for hers.

"Lauren, oh shit, fuck, shit! I didn't mean, this wasn't…" Lucy cried as she tried to pull her dress on. She tripped and landed on her knees. "Oh god," she sobbed, her eyes pleading with Lauren.

Lauren shook her head, narrowing her eyes between Lucy and Nick. "I can't believe this. You… you… slut!" Lauren screamed, tears streaming down her face. Nick snapped his head up and looked ashamed.

Yes, Alex was her brother, and witnessing Lucy cheating on him was shocking, but deep down Lauren knew that wasn't the real reason she was so upset. It was logical to be mad, of course, but the emotions she was experiencing were so much deeper than that.

"No, Lauren, I... I swear this has never happened before!" Lucy staggered around, trying to put her shoes on as Lauren bolted out the door and half ran–half fell down the stairs. "I'm sorry! Wait, Lauren!"

24

Lucy picked up her phone to see who was texting. Alex was sprawled out on her bed watching videos on his own phone, so she discretely clicked on the text from Nick, her eyes flickering back and forth between the screen and Alex.

NICK: You going to Chelsea's party?

LUCY: Why are you texting me?

NICK: Bcuz, senior year is almost over. IDK why I can't let it go, but I just can't. What if we just snuck away and saw what it was like?

LUCY: What what was like?

NICK: Us, being together.

Alex laughed out loud at a video he was watching. Lucy jumped, dropping her phone in her lap. Alex looked up and grinned, tipping his phone towards her so she could see the video of some guy falling off his bicycle down a hill. Even though she thought those types of videos were idiotic, she forced a smile. Alex guffawed loudly as he watched it again then went back to scrolling.

She'd once thought his goofy appreciation for things like that was adorable. Once, she'd loved his boyish sense of humor. But Alex seemed to be taking senior year as a personal challenge to get as drunk as he could as many times as he could while behaving in the most outrageous way at every party. None of it had been dangerous per se, but the stupid pranks and stunts weren't funny anymore. She was tired of cleaning up after a sloppy drunk boyfriend. And she couldn't forget the party where he'd kissed some girl from the junior class. Okay, so they'd both been completely wasted, and Lucy wasn't even sure Alex was conscious when it had happened—she'd walked in and found them on the couch, lips pressed together. Alex hadn't even seemed aware that anyone was kissing him, much less who. So, Lucy had forgiven him and let it go. Mostly.

She picked her phone back up and saw another message.

NICK: You still there? It would be easy. Alex will be wasted, it's our chance.

LUCY: It'd be such a mistake.

NICK: I know you feel what I've been feeling.

LUCY: It's lust, Nick. Stupid teenage hormones.

NICK: Yeah, but do you feel that with Alex?

Lucy's eyes flicked over to Alex. She knew the answer. She'd been denying it because Alex was a big football star. And graduation was coming up—she didn't want to rock the boat now, not at the end of the year. The fallout would be too much. It'd be pointless. She was going off to college soon.

At one point, she'd really thought she was in love with Alex. Those feelings had dwindled and turned to disgust and annoyance, but even so she was willing to hold out and play the part for one more month. Sighing, she glanced down as another message popped up.

NICK: Well, do you?

Lucy's fingers hovered over the screen, shaking. With a quick exhale, she typed.

LUCY: Fine. One night. After Alex is drunk. But we never tell anyone, and then we go our separate ways.

NICK: Sure.

LUCY: I mean it.

NICK: Okay, yeah.

Nerves bubbled up in Lucy's stomach, and she glanced at Alex again. She couldn't believe what she'd just agreed to.

But… part of her *was* curious. A big part of her. She decided then and there not to deny that what she wanted was to play the field. She was hungry for the school year to end and for college to begin. She couldn't wait to be away from this town, to explore other feelings, have adventures, new experiences.

Her gaze wandered back to Alex. She paused, wondering if she would let herself get tied down to someone else like she'd done with him.

The thought sobered her. She straightened, making a silent promise to herself that she would date around and enjoy experiencing different partners at college. She wouldn't lock herself down to one person. Certainly not someone she didn't even like.

For just a moment, Lucy allowed herself to feel excited about what she was going to do. Yes, it was cheating, sneaky and wrong. But wasn't that what high school was for? Making mistakes?

25

FIVE YEARS BEFORE
GAME NIGHT

Justin glanced at his phone ringing on the coffee table in front of him. Reaching for the remote, he paused the show he was watching. It was late for his mother to be calling him, but he already knew why. He was surprised it had taken her so long.

"Hello?"

His mother immediately took a long exaggerated breath. "Justin, have you seen the news?" she asked, her voice breaking. This made Justin pause. He wasn't sure what reaction he'd expected her to have, but he certainly hadn't expected her to have been crying her heart out.

"What news? I worked late today." He didn't know why he was playing dumb, but if he admitted he'd already heard, his mother would ask why he hadn't called her immediately.

"It's Troy. He's dead." A sob rippled through the phone line.

Justin measured his response carefully. "I'm sorry, Mom. Are you okay? What happened?" he asked, but the words hung between them.

His mother had divorced Troy shortly after he'd graduated high school, and she'd since moved on and was happily married to another man. At least... he thought they were happy.

She sniffed hard, disrupting his train of thought. "I'm okay, yeah. I think it's just a shock. I don't really know why I'm crying so much," she said around sobs, and Justin exhaled a sigh of relief.

"They think he was killed by an intruder. Roy said..." She paused and blew her nose. Justin sat up straighter. His mother's new husband, Roy, worked for the PD. Justin wondered what he knew.

"Roy said what, Mom?" Justin tried to quell his impatience, but he needed to know.

"They think it might have been drug related, but it seems like he was taken by surprise. Stabbed to death, but his house was loaded with drugs," his mother said, her crying finally subsiding.

"Wow," was all Justin could say because it'd been expected. His tone lacked the surprise it should have held, and a long silence followed. Justin waited.

"Justin, you haven't seen or talked to Troy lately, have you?" she asked.

Justin's stomach dropped, not at the question but at her tone. Her insinuation was clear. "No, of course not," he answered, guilt dancing around his half-truths. He heard her audible sigh of relief. Part of him wished he could tell her everything, but it would be too much for her. It would destroy her. So they were his secrets to keep. *Does she suspect I was involved with Troy's death?*

"Oh, it looks like Roy's home. He just pulled up. He's been so good about this, but I don't want him to see my crying over my ex again. I need to go. We'll talk soon. Love you," his mom said, ending the call before he could even respond.

Justin immediately went to the browser on his phone and searched for the story again. He wanted to see if there were any new public details. None of the articles he'd found mentioned drugs; they'd all mentioned an intruder and alluded to possible burglary. He didn't know if someone was covering for Troy or if they were just keeping the details confidential while they investigated.

Troy's death might have brought a new weight to bear, but it had also brought a sense of relief.

26

GAME NIGHT

"These games are getting boring. Let's play something else," Alex said, barely able to sit up straight. Lucy glanced at him and gave her head a minimal shake before looking around at the others.

Justin wiped his hands on his pant legs and reached for another drink. "Sure, what did you have in mind?"

"How about, shpin the bottle?" Alex waggled his eyebrows and then guffawed loudly, snorting and sending himself into another fit of drunken laughs.

Lauren made a gagging sound and shot him a look. "Gross, Alex."

"Oh shorry, not with my shitser, though."

"Woah, let's get him some water," Lucy said, concern shadowing her face as she started to get up from the couch.

"I'll grab him a bottle," Hannah offered, darting in and out of the kitchen in a flash before Lucy could even stand up. She brought the water bottle to Alex, opening it and handing it over.

"Okay, so not shpin the bottle, but one of those other games. Whatdya think about 'would you ever?'" Alex talked slowly, as though his tongue had grown ten times its normal size. He tipped the water bottle back, and Lucy watched as it trickled out of the corners of his mouth, dripping onto his shirt. She looked away, embarrassed for him.

"You mean 'Never Have I Ever?'" Hannah perched on the edge of an armchair, her interest suddenly piqued.

"Uh, yeah sure." Alex shrugged, staring at the water bottle in his hand like he just realized he had it. "This vodka is good." As he took another drink, nervous laughs quickly died out. The last time they'd seen him so drunk, it hadn't ended well.

"Okay, so how should we start?" Hannah asked, sitting up straight, knees tucked together, back rigid. After another minute, she clapped her hands together. "Ooo! I have an idea!" Her excitement was met with awkward smiles.

Justin looked grateful that someone else was taking charge. He relaxed back in his chair a little.

"What's your idea?" Lauren asked, her eyebrows lifting with feigned interest.

Lucy smiled to herself, recognizing Lauren's artificial curiosity. Some things never changed; once the nice girl, always the nice girl.

Jumping up, Hannah squealed. "What if we all jot down a few 'Never Have I Ever's' on slips of paper and throw them in a bowl?" After digging around in the end table drawer, she pulled out a notepad and a few pens. She tore the paper into strips and handed each person a few along with a pen. Lucy wanted to protest, but found the words stuck in her throat, not wanting to squash her hostess's enthusiasm.

"Write one thing on each slip of paper. Then we'll draw them out and read them. If you've done it, you have to drink!" Hannah clapped her hands together, the loud smack causing the others to jump. "Does anyone need a refill?" She seemed determined to pump some fun back into the gathering though, so they all reached for pens and started writing.

Hannah went back to the kitchen for a bowl while everyone started writing, the occasional giggle or snort breaking the silence. Lucy tapped her pen on her lips and quickly started writing. She folded her papers up in tiny squares and waited for Hannah to swoop by with the bowl before tossing hers in.

"Perfect, let's start!" Hannah announced as the last papers were dropped into the bowl. The room hummed with anticipation.

"I'll go first," Nick said, reaching into the bowl and plucking out a strip of paper with panache. Clearing his throat, he began reading stoically. "I've never owned a dog." Nick rolled his eyes. Taking a quick drink, he tossed the used paper on the table.

"Who put that lame one in there?" Alex asked, sounding a little more sober. The others chuckled and looked around until their eyes landed on Hannah.

She shrugged it off with a smile. "I've never had a dog… and I don't want to get drunk too fast!"

"You go next," Lucy said, nerves dancing in her belly like electrified butterflies. The stakes for this game were potentially high—some of those slips could reveal big secrets.

"Never have I ever…" Hannah began, pausing dramatically and looking at the slip of paper, "Cheated on someone." Groans echoed between them as everyone's eyes darted around.

Finally, Lucy shrugged. "Well, I guess I'll drink."

Alex and Nick took a big gulp and then turned to Justin, who shook his head no, and then Hannah who also shook her head. Turning last to Lauren, they watched as she took a drink.

Lucy gasped. "Lauren!" Maybe she wasn't the Lauren Lucy remembered. She studied Lauren's face, suddenly a lot more interested.

Lauren looked down at her drink, refusing to meet their gazes. "Shit happens, right?" she mumbled, reaching into the bowl and grabbing a slip of paper before anyone could ask more questions.

"Never have I ever slept with my boss to get ahead," Lauren read before tossing the paper on the table, looking relieved.

"Nope," Alex snorted while Nick and Justin shook their heads.

"I considered it!" Lucy laughed, but they all stopped when they realized Hannah was taking a drink. Her face was flushed, and she refused to meet their gazes.

Alex whistled low.

"Really?" Justin asked, sitting more alert. It was clear he hadn't known.

"Well, I was young, so it wasn't really a conscious

choice—like I didn't necessarily think I was just sleeping with her to get a promotion, but it did get me one." Embarrassment flooded her face, but she pressed on. "Live and learn, right?" She shrugged, cringing.

"Her?" Justin repeated.

"Close your mouth, bro," Nick joked, leaning forward to slap Justin's arm.

"I didn't know any of that. Are you…"

"Am I what? Bisexual? Yes, I am. I thought you knew," Hannah said, her forehead furrowed.

"Well, I do now. It's fine. I mean, of course it's fine. I just… didn't know," Justin fumbled. Lucy and Lauren locked eyes for a moment while Hannah and Justin whisper-bickered back and forth.

Something stirred inside Lucy, an abandoned sense of longing returning. She couldn't take her eyes off Lauren, suddenly wanting to burst into tears. She fought back the feeling and forced herself to focus on the game.

"Okay, well you guys can sort that out later. I'll go." Alex grabbed a slip of paper and started reading. "I've never thrown up after a meal," he said, his voice suddenly too loud in a room that had become too quiet. "On purpose."

All attention turned to Lucy.

Lucy took a drink and then forced a laugh. "But what woman hasn't at some point? Am I right?" she asked, looking pointedly at Lauren and Hannah. They traded awkward glances but both shook their heads. Lucy swallowed hard, heat rising up her neck. She should have lied. Now she looked like the trainwreck she knew she was.

"No, Lucy, I've never done that. That's… not healthy," Lauren said gently.

Lucy stared at her for a moment but quickly looked away as her eyes began to water. *Do not cry. Do not cry!*

Hannah reached over and put her hand on Lucy's. "Oh honey, is that why you're so thin?"

Justin gasped while the rest of the group froze with mouths gaping open like fish out of water. Lucy lowered her lashes, staring at her lap, the room turning fuzzy. Peering back up, faces were blurry.

"Dang, whoever wrote that, that's just not right," Nick said. He glanced at the others, seemingly trying to read their expressions. But they all appeared just as appalled.

Lucy avoided eye contact with the others, hers burning with unshed tears. Her worst secret had just been revealed, and everyone thought she was disgusting.

27

GAME NIGHT

lex's game provided the kind of luck that I could have kissed someone for. The perfect way to up the ante of the night. I knew secrets. Everyone's secrets. Things they wouldn't want to admit. It didn't matter that I hadn't spoken to any of them over the last ten years. I'd been watching. Waiting.

I couldn't believe the opportunity that landed right in my lap. I wrote fast, so no one would realize how many slips I was filling out. I let everything loose. Their darkest secrets, all laid out for everyone to know now.

I'd always hated games like this, but I wasn't about to throw away my chance to revel in the chaos. Make everyone uncomfortable. Humiliate them. Demonstrate what horrible people they were. .

Cowards, every last one.

28

TWO WEEKS BEFORE
GAME NIGHT

Lucy squirmed in her seat, looking around the table at her co-workers. After stuffing themselves with appetizers and the soup and salad that had followed, they now dove into their main courses. Uninhibited, carefree and lubricated by drink after drink.

Lucy had deftly declined the appetizers and merely picked at her salad. But now was the hard part. The decadent plate of white fish and rice with roasted vegetables sat in front of her, tempting her. Eating was inevitable.

"That looks delicious!" one of the accountants said, pointing at Lucy's plate before diving into his steak.

Lucy smiled and picked up her fork, raking it through the rice, exercising restraint, reminding herself not to partake. Her stomach growled. Clearing her throat to cover the sound, she expertly sectioned the fish. Usually the components of this dish were on her list of 'safe foods,' but she imagined they'd been cooked in a pan full of butter.

Cheryl, an older co-worker, nudged her. "Everything okay?" she whispered, her mouth turned down with concern.

"Oh yes," Lucy answered, pulling her lips into a smile. "I just had a late lunch. I didn't realize I'd still be so full."

Cheryl watched her a moment longer before nodding, turning back to her own plate, and rejoining the conversation.

Forcing herself to take tiny bites, Lucy flaked off pieces of the fish, moving the food around so it looked like she'd eaten. If she moved slowly enough, someone would come by and sweep the plates away. Her stomach growled again, and she shifted uncomfortably in her seat.

"What about you, Lucy? Did you have any new ideas for our community involvement campaign?" her boss, Morgan, asked.

It was hard to concentrate, hunger making her weak. So stupid, she scolded herself. She'd forgotten about this mandatory dinner meeting today, and she hadn't packed a lunch. Most days, she was content with black coffee for breakfast and no lunch. When she got home, she'd make herself a small, bland meal. Having control over how it was cooked helped keep the guilt at bay.

She took a long drink of water, her hand shaking.

Cheryl glanced over again. "Lucy's just being shy. She had a really great idea that she ran by me earlier."

Caught off guard, Lucy's fork paused. She'd been in a fog all day. She hadn't been able to think of one idea that someone else hadn't already suggested. She certainly hadn't told Cheryl about one.

"So, Lucy, would you like to share the idea with everyone then?" Morgan prompted, looking at her expectantly.

"Oh I'm sorry," Lucy stuttered, feeling dizzy. She blinked and set her fork down. "I wasn't quite ready to present it to everyone just yet. I wanted to do some research first…" She took another sip. Although she could feel Morgan's steady gaze on her, she refused to make eye contact.

"Well, that's what this dinner is all about," Morgan said. "Brainstorming. No need for formal pitches. We're here to hash out ideas."

Everything went fuzzy. Morgan's mouth was moving, but Lucy's surroundings were a blur. She felt woozy. She'd finally reached the point where she had to eat something or she would pass out in the middle of this meeting.

But Morgan was staring at her, expecting a response.

Lucy swallowed and tried to slow her rapid pulse. Once again, Cheryl stepped in and saved her. Filled with gratitude, Lucy barely kept the tears from falling.

"Lucy's being bashful because her idea's a little bit out there. But I don't mind spilling the beans!" Cheryl, with her bright makeup, garish red hair and matching nails, had everyone's full attention. Everyone, that is, except Morgan, who was watching Lucy with a mixture of annoyance and concern.

Lucy shoveled in a big bite, as much for nourishment as an excuse to not speak. She certainly didn't need to black out. Not that it would've been the first time.

Lost in the ceremony of eating, Lucy didn't hear

another word Cheryl said. Instead, she scarfed down every last morsel on her plate. When she finished, the waiter brought dessert. Lucy normally declined, claiming she was full from the meal, but tonight she pulled the plate towards her and devoured it.

Cheryl finished detailing "Lucy's plan," and their colleagues prattled on about what a great idea it was, throwing undeserved praise Lucy's way.

Lucy glanced up and saw that everyone was watching her, just as a piece of cheesecake crust stuck to the corner of her mouth. She wiped it away, suddenly nauseous. Cheryl was beaming and nodding, urging Lucy to accept the praise that was rightfully Cheryl's.

Lucy opened her mouth, ready to share credit for Cheryl's idea—though she had no clue what the idea was —but when she did, she realized she was going to be sick.

"I'm so sorry, I don't feel well," she blurted, grabbing her purse from the back of the chair and bolting for the bathroom.

Slamming the stall door closed behind her, she crouched in front of the toilet bowl and emptied her stomach. When she was finished, she flushed and then sat on the seat to dig through her purse for a wipe. Pulling out her compact mirror, she dabbed her face carefully. Then stared at herself. *Pathetic.*

The bathroom door banged open. Lucy pulled her feet up so no one would see her shoes and froze.

"Lucy? Are you in here?"

Lucy's stomach lurched at the sound of Morgan's voice. She held her breath, steadying herself until finally the door swung shut. Lucy's phone dinged, and she scrambled to grab it out of her purse.

The text was from Morgan asking if she was okay. She told Lucy it was fine if she went home sick, that they would discuss her idea the next day in the office.

Lucy breathed a sigh of relief but didn't bother responding. She tucked her phone back into her purse, exited the bathroom, and slipped out of the restaurant before anyone spotted her.

On the way to her car, she made a plan. She'd show up at the office the next day and pretend nothing had happened. If anyone dared to ask, she would claim that the fish must have been bad. It was a safe complaint since no one else had ordered it.

Lucy paused for a moment, key poised at the lock, thinking about all the lies. Her body and her eating habits were the only aspect of her life that she had complete control over. What had started as a way to punish herself for what happened ten years ago, had evolved into her way of coping.

When all else was spiraling out of control, at least she had this. At least she could control *something*.

29

SENIOR PARTY

L auren's head spun as she pushed her way through a group of kids lingering around. The music was pounding, making it hard for her to think. She had just one mission: find Alex.

Her vision blurred—not only because she'd drunk more than she ever had, but also thanks to the burning tears that threatened to fall. Tears over the betrayal lodged deep in her gut. She could still hear Lucy calling her name, trying to catch up.

Lauren trudged forward. Her heart raced, and she pushed past the sweaty drunk bodies swaying to the music. She ran headfirst into Hazel, who asked about Justin and Shane. Lauren pushed her out of the way.

"Lauren, where are you going?" Hazel asked, but

Lauren didn't pause. She moved faster and faster until she burst out onto the patio.

Alex.

He was standing alone at the edge of the pool, swaying to the music, lost in his own drunken stupor. Carefree.

Her heart sank. She was about to burst that bubble. Her feet skidded to a stop. *Maybe I shouldn't. Maybe I should let him be. After all, ignorance is bliss, right?*

"Lauren!" Alex shouted, his grin widening. He held his arms out as he stepped towards her. She fell into her brother's arms and melted into one of his monstrous brother hugs.

"Isn't this the greatest night?" he said, oblivious to her trembling. She pulled back. He caught her face, red and pinched, tears watering her eyes.

"Oh hey, what's wrong? What happened?" His words garbled together, as though his tongue was too heavy.

Even Drunk Alex was the best big brother. Lauren knew he could be a douchebag in a lot of ways, but he was nothing if not a protective brother.

"I–Alex, it's Lucy. She—" Lauren hesitated, realizing just how drunk she was. She tried to steady herself by leaning on Alex, but he was swaying too. Everything spun around her.

"Lucy? What's wrong with Lucy?" Alex asked while Lauren gripped his arm.

"I don't know if I should be telling you, but I saw Lucy with–"

"Lauren, not now!" Lucy shrieked.

Alex turned as Lucy stumbled up to them, her hair a wild mess. His nose crinkled, his face a mask of confusion. Lauren knew he wasn't the fastest at picking up on things, but drunk… he was clearly lost.

"With who?" Alex asked.

Nick approached but hung back.

Alex locked eyes with Nick. "Tell me, Lauren," Alex demanded, his jaw clenching.

He might be drunk and normally oblivious, but Lauren recognized the spark behind his eyes. Maybe he already knew what she was going to say.

"Lucy and Nick," Lauren squeaked and stepped away from Lucy who had been squeezing her arm. Lauren glanced down at the fingernail marks left behind. She realized she'd just betrayed her best friend. *But Lucy stabbed me in the back too.*

Realization spread across Alex's face. "What were Lucy and Nick doing?" Alex's tone flatlined and turned deathly quiet. He cracked his knuckles and held Nick's gaze. Nick visibly swallowed.

"I feel sick," Lucy cried, leaning over the edge of the patio to empty her stomach.

Lauren furrowed her brows, wondering if she had made a mistake. *Of course you made a mistake!* She was too drunk to think clearly. She shouldn't have told Alex tonight. Maybe not ever. She shivered despite the humidity.

"You made a move on my girlfriend?" Alex asked, incredulous. "When she was drunk?" He stepped closer and tapped his hand against Nick's chest.

Nick stumbled back. "I… it wasn't like that," he muttered.

"We hooked up, Alex. I'm sorry," Lucy said, walking up to him, her stance defiant.

"Hooked up?" Alex growled, swiveling around to look at her, almost losing his balance.

In the face of his anger, Lucy looked down at her shoes. "Yes."

"What exactly does 'hooked up' mean?"

"Alex. You know what it means." Lucy looked up at him, regret etching every feature of her face.

Alex's mouth opened and closed like a fish out of water as he grappled with what she was saying. "As in... you–you did... you had... But we don't even...!" Alex shouted, struggling to find the words. "I can't believe it. My girlfriend and my best friend. You guys suck!" Alex roared.

Lauren reached out for Alex's arm, recognizing the anger was only masking the hurt, but he shrugged her off.

"I'm out of here," he said, storming off towards their vehicles.

"Alex, wait!" Lucy called, chasing after him.

"Fuck," Nick spat and turned to Lauren..

"Wait! Alex" Lauren joined Lucy and raced after her brother.

30

THREE MONTHS BEFORE
GAME NIGHT

lex's head was pounding. Heat crept up the back of his neck, his heart racing as he walked down the hall towards the conference room. The lights overhead flickered and cast a glow that seemed to echo the sick feeling in his stomach.

He was hanging on by a thread. His suit was damp with sweat and dingy, reflecting his confidence level. What had once been a crisp white shirt was now crinkled, stained, and smelled faintly of beer and cigarette smoke. His pants, barely buttoning, were wrinkled and discolored. Scuff marks covered his shoes. His external appearance matched his insides; at last he had hit rock bottom, and he knew it.

It had been a long week, longer than usual. He could

barely remember half of it. Fragments and flashes of moments, faces, conversations—most of them blurred, all clouded by the haze of alcohol. And now, the inevitable was upon him.

The door to the conference room swung open with a creak, and Alex stepped inside, taking his seat without saying a word. The tension in the room was palpable, thick enough to suffocate him. Miranda, the HR manager, sat at the head of the long rectangular table. Across from her were two others: Jordan, his manager, and Jeannie, a senior colleague from the legal department. They didn't look up when he entered.

Alex fidgeted, shifting back and forth, his hands tucked under his knees, trying to steady his breath. He had a vague idea of what was about to happen. The warning signs had been there for weeks, months even. A missed deadline here, an inappropriate comment brushed off there, a glance, a whisper behind his back. It had all caught up to him. Today, they were all wearing that *look*. Disappointment. The look that meant this was the end.

"Alex," Miranda began, voice calm, demeanor cold. She lifted her eyes to meet his. The quiet rustle of paper made the silence even more uncomfortable. "We've asked you to come here today to discuss some serious concerns regarding your behavior at work."

Alex tried to swallow, but his throat was so dry he ended up gasping for breath. Despite knowing this was coming, he felt himself unraveling quickly.

"Okay," he stuttered. The last few months had been a blur of late nights at the bar, foggy workdays, and strained interactions with colleagues. What had they seen? What had they heard? Could they be talking about the incident last week? No, that couldn't be it. Could it?

Miranda continued, her voice unwavering. "We've had multiple complaints filed against you, Alex. These complaints have come from your colleagues, and we've conducted a thorough investigation."

The room spun. His mind shifted through moments that had stood out over the past few months. Flashes of laughter at the office happy hours, the quick exchanges with coworkers as they shuffled past him in the hallway, the drunken texts, the awkward conversations where he'd found himself stumbling over words. He knew his work had been sloppy… and his behavior borderline illegal.

He wanted to speak up, to explain, but his mouth felt glued shut. He closed his eyes against the harsh fluorescent lights, willing the contents of his stomach to stay down.

"The complaints against you involve inappropriate behavior towards several female colleagues," Miranda went on, her tone clinical, detached. "There have been instances where you have made them feel uncomfortable, unsafe even. The latest report crosses a line."

Alex's mind flooded with all of the interactions he could recall. The happy hours that extended into something else. His mind scanned through them all, wondering who had complained. *Megan.* It had to be Megan. Megan, who reminded him so much of Lucy. He knew when he had too many drinks, he was prone to being too pushy. But they'd been at a bar after work… What did that have to do with work?

"I didn't mean…" Alex started, but his voice trailed off,

a hollow sound that seemed to fade before it could reach anyone's ears.

Jordan, his manager, shifted in his seat, his eyes narrowing as he glanced up from his notepad. Alex hadn't even thought he was listening.

"Alex, these aren't isolated incidents," Jordan said, and Alex's stomach clenched. "This is a pattern of behavior that we can no longer ignore. You've crossed boundaries, and there are now serious concerns about your judgment and conduct in the workplace."

Alex's face flushed scarlet. His chest tightened. "I was just... just trying to be friendly," Alex mumbled, his words stumbling over one another. "I didn't mean anything by it. Lots of us have been out drinking and having fun together. You know how it is. Come on, I've been here for years. No one's complained before..."

Jeannie, from legal, cleared her throat, cutting him off. Her back was rigid, and her lips pursed. Alex knew she was a no-nonsense partner who didn't back down from confrontation. He'd always admired that quality in the past, but now that it was directed at him, he hated it.

"It's not just the comments, Alex. It's also your behavior outside of these incidents. We're aware of your drinking problem, and it's been affecting your performance here. We've received complaints about your behavior during work hours, the way you've been showing up late, and the state you've been in during meetings."

His heart sank. He'd been trying to ignore that aspect —the drinking that had gotten way out of hand. He kept promising himself he wouldn't drink during the work day anymore, or so late at night that he was still drunk the next morning. But he broke those promises over and over. He had to drink, he couldn't get through a single day without guilt eating away at him.

"You've been given warnings, and I'm sorry it's come to this." Miranda's choice of words made his stomach lurch.

Jordan spoke again. "Alex, we've made the decision to terminate your employment. Effective immediately. We'll provide you with the necessary severance, but you'll need to leave the office today."

Alex struggled to compose himself, the room tilting. He swallowed hard, forcing down the bile. "I understand. I'll get my things," he said, his voice somehow devoid of emotion. He jerked out of the seat and fled to his small office, thankful for a moment of privacy. He didn't need to look behind him to know that they'd followed and were waiting in the hall to make sure he turned in his badge and exited peacefully.

Glancing around his office, he realized they'd already removed company files and equipment. There was an empty box on his desk for him to pack what few personal effects he had. He didn't keep much at work, certainly nothing of value, so he simply tossed the few things he had into the trash. He dropped his badge on his desk and turned to leave.

Jordan blocked the doorway but after seeing the badge on the desk, he let Alex slip past him. Alex walked at a brisk pace past the cubicles and the reception desk and fled from the building as quickly as he could, desperate to escape prying eyes.

31

GAME NIGHT

"Whatever, this game is stupid," Lauren said, flopping back, crossing her arms, and glaring at the group.

"Hey, it's better than those damn board games." Alex gestured towards the stack they had abandoned. "Let's just keep playing. Who cares if one person decided to write something stupid? Isn't the point to reveal secrets?" Alex blurted out but then realized what he'd said. "You go next, Justin," he added quickly. He certainly didn't want *his* big secret to be revealed…

"Never have I ever," Justin began, "gotten fired for sexual harassment. Oh damn." Justin set his glass down and looked around.

Alex, in true Alex form, snorted with laughter. *Fuck it.* He took a dramatic gulp while everyone stared.

Lauren's mouth hung open. "What job was that?" she screeched. Alex ignored the eyes darting towards him and pretended his sister wasn't burning a hole through him with her stare.

Refusing to answer, he gestured towards the bowl containing the slips of paper. "Next!" Alex avoided his sister's gaze.

"No, Alex, I want to know. When was this? What job? You've only had a couple of serious jobs since college. You got fired? Are you *unemployed* right now?" The word was said with such distaste that Alex visibly flinched. Her question hung in the air, and everyone shifted uncomfortably.

Alex's eyes darted around the room. No one said anything, and they averted their gazes. He heaved a large sigh, giving in and offering somewhat of an explanation.

"Yeah, okay, my perfect job is gone. I got fired. I don't even know what I did. A bunch of us went out for drinks... a lot. Then someone complained about me. I thought we were all just having fun, and yeah, I was wasted. But really, who knows? Maybe *I* was taken advantage of. Maybe *they* wanted to turn the tables on *me*." His allegation seemed to fall on deaf ears, making him all the more defensive and irritable. "Whatever. All I know is they ganged up on me, and I'm out. Okay?" Alex spat, snatching a slip of paper from the bowl with such aggression, the bowl teetered on the edge of the table before Hannah caught it.

"How long ago was that?" Lauren asked, clearly not willing to let it go until she had all the answers.

"Geez, L! I don't know! A few months. But who cares? The whole point of this fucking game is to reveal our secrets and make us look bad. So there it is. I don't know which one of you knew, but yes, I fucked up, and that's that."

The silence that followed stretched across them like a spider web. No one seemed to know how to respond.

Justin cleared his throat. All eyes turned to him as if to see what their host would do to diffuse the situation.

Alex tried to clear his head—the alcohol slowed his thinking. *Shit, who knew about what happened?* He hadn't told anyone, so that had to mean rumors had spread from someone at the company. Eager to move the conversation along, Alex pressed on.

"Who cares? Let's move on and put someone else in the hot seat. I need to keep drinking, so let's see what this one says." Alex unfolded the paper and breathed a sigh of relief.

Reading aloud like a game-show host, he stared at Nick. "I've never proposed to my boss's daughter for a promotion."

"What the fuck? Who wrote that?" Lauren asked, snatching the paper from Alex. Anyone could have written it, Alex felt like telling her. It was scrolled in neat yet indistinctive block letters.

"Anyone could have assumed that, I guess. I mean, sorry bro, but she's not exactly a looker." Alex realized he had said this out loud rather than just in his head when echoes of disapproval and shocked expressions circled the group.

"Dude, that's just wrong," Justin said to Alex, but even he didn't take his eyes off of Nick. No one had taken a drink, but as the time stretched, Nick lifted his glass to his lips and tipped it back, his throat bobbing with a deep swallow.

"So, it's true?" Lucy's eyelashes fluttered. "That's… I can't believe it. You wouldn't…" She shook her head in denial.

He wouldn't? Alex tried to hide his scoff. *It's not the first time Nick did something I didn't think he would do.*

Nick's shoulders slumped. "I kind of got cornered. Or threatened, I guess? I didn't propose for the promotion, even though I did get one."

"Then why?"

Nick sighed. "Because my boss hinted that if I didn't, he would destroy me and my career. Alicia's a nice girl, but… yeah, that's the truth of it."

Alex let out a low whistle. So he wasn't the only one with work issues.

"You can't marry someone you don't love!" Lucy shouted.

Well, well, well. Someone still cares more about Nick than she should. Alex bit his tongue.

Nick chuffed and shook his head, keeping his sights on Lucy. "I don't know that it matters. I mean, I haven't been in love with anyone since–"

Lauren cut him off. "Hey, let's take a break, huh? This is getting kinda heavy." Her eyes darted towards Alex.

Thanks, sis. Good save.

"Yeah, sure," Hannah said, standing and clearing her throat. She began gathering empty cups. "Does anyone want me to grab them another drink?"

Justin nodded. "Sure, let's do another round." Justin looked relieved.

Maybe none of our lives turned out the way we had hoped.

32

ONE MONTH BEFORE
GAME NIGHT

Ralph Goldberg was a short, stout man with a wobbly second chin. His cartoon-like appearance should have made him less of a threat but for Nick, being in the presence of his boss always made him anxious.

Last year, Ralph had bullied Nick into taking his daughter on a date. When Alicia fell for Nick, Ralph made it clear that if Nick hurt her, he wouldn't have a job or any place in the industry. Ralph's influence in the business stretched further than Nick cared to think about. Having seen Ralph destroy former employees' livelihoods with just a couple phone calls, Nick constantly worried about fucking things up.

So when Ralph's email popped up requesting Nick

stop by his office for "a drink, man to man," Nick's legs turned to jelly, and his guts quivered. He knew he was about to receive direct orders disguised as a simple request.

When 5:00 p.m. rolled around, Nick rose from his desk and dropped his cell phone and keys in his pocket. Each step down the hallway felt like a nail in his coffin, reverberating in his chest. He wished he hadn't eaten lunch, because it was threatening to make a reprise.

Stopping in front of the imposing mahogany door, he wondered what Ralph could possibly want. All of his accounts were in order. His clients, all satisfied. Had he missed something? Had someone lodged a complaint?

Nick raised a reluctant and trembling hand to knock. He shook it out, trying to quell his nerves. It wouldn't bode well for him to show weakness. He wished he could have prepared a defense, but he truly didn't know what he was walking into. *It's no use.* He was here now and had no choice but to go in.

He knocked and waited for Ralph's response before opening the door and stepping in.

"Nick!" Ralph said, his unusual sense of enthusiasm rising him off his chair with arms spread wide.

Nick closed the door behind him and fought to keep the surprise from showing. *This is going to be worse than what I thought.* He would rather be reprimanded. Based on the way Ralph was grinning and welcoming him in, he was pretty sure he was about to be asked to do a "favor" of sorts. Some kind of shady business deal he needed help with. Classic Ralph style.

"Have a seat, son." Ralph gestured to the chair across from his desk, and Nick lowered himself uneasily. Ralph nudged a glass of whiskey towards him. Ralph lifted his and tipped it in a salute. Uncertainty buzzed throughout Nick's body, but he returned the gesture and took a long swallow. It burned all the way down to his already sour stomach, and he fought the urge to grimace.

"So how can I help you, Mr. Goldberg?" Nick asked formally, sitting up straight in the chair, not wanting to let his guard down.

"Oh Nick, call me Ralph." His boisterous laugh made Nick jump. Every hair on his neck stood at attention, indicating something was about to happen. Something that would perhaps change his life forever.

"Okay," Nick said slowly.

"You look nervous, son. Relax. This is a good meeting! I wanted to talk about my daughter."

Nick stilled in his seat. He hadn't expected that. "Alicia?" Nick's voice broke from nerves. He chastised himself for sounding like a scared little brat.

Ralph shot him a condescending smirk and raised his eyebrows. "Is there another? Of course Alicia. You've been dating my daughter for a year now. How do you think it's going?" he asked, leaning forward and propping his arms up on his desk.

Nick paused and set his glass down before wiping his hands on his pant legs. "It's good. She's a great girl." Nick bobbed his head, anticipating the direction of the conversation. His stomach rolled, and he clenched his teeth, willing the nausea away.

"Yes, yes. I know that." Ralph waved his hand in front of him. "I'm wondering about next steps."

Nick fumbled for the right words. What he wanted to say was that he wasn't in love and hadn't been since high school. That no one would ever hold a candle to the way he felt about Lucy. Logically, he knew it was ridiculous to still be holding a flame for a high school crush. Even so, hope that one day he'd meet someone to make him forget clung to him. But he knew it wasn't Alicia.

Nick cleared his throat. "Alicia and I talked about her moving in, but she thought you would want a ring on her finger first."

"I see." Ralph sat back, a sly smile finding his face. He linked his hands together and dropped them on his generous belly. His foot tapped beneath the desk.

"I figured you couldn't afford a ring that meets Alicia's standards, so I thought I'd help you out."

Nick forced his face to remain neutral even though his insides were screaming *"It's a trap!"*

Ralph opened the side drawer of his desk and pulled out a small jewelry box. He opened it and showed Nick one of the most ridiculous and gaudy engagement rings he'd ever seen. Nick blinked, unable to respond.

"I want you to have this, for Alicia of course. She's ready for that next step." Ralph slid the box across his desk. When Nick didn't move, Ralph's proud smirk turned into a scowl.

"You're up for a promotion. It would be... beneficial for a man about to be married to secure that position. Don't you agree?" Ralph narrowed his eyes. "I can't think of anything worse than for a single man to lose his job *and* have his name dragged through the mud. Can you?" His eyes didn't leave Nick.

Nick fought the urge to wipe away the beads of sweat gathering at his hairline. "It's a very generous offer, sir. I'm just not sure it's right," Nick said, gesturing towards the box. "I should pick out and purchase an engagement ring myself," he said, stalling for time.

Ralph visibly relaxed, the veins in his temples melding back into place. "I suppose. *If* that was important in the long run. But I don't really see how that matters. It's more important that Alicia be happy with the ring she gets, wouldn't you agree?"

Nick was at a loss for what to say or do. After a couple of tries, he managed to answer with a shaky, "Yes?"

"Great! I made reservations for the two of you at Alahambra's for seven on Friday night. You'll have the rooftop dining area to yourselves; I've already requested a violinist and flowers. All you have to do is wear a suit, bring this ring, and ask one simple question." He stood and walked around the desk to set the box directly in front of Nick. "Don't you hurt my girl, Nick."

Nick's mind raced, but he couldn't see a way out. There wasn't one simple thing about it. And his hands were tied.

After Nick picked up the ring, Ralph ended the meeting and ushered Nick out before anything else could be discussed.

One week later, Alicia moved in.

33

GAME NIGHT

annah carried the tray of refilled drinks back to the room, and everyone reached for a glass.

"I need to use the bathroom." Lucy stood up, looking at Hannah since she didn't know where to go.

"Oh sure, let me show you. You'll need to use the one upstairs, because the downstairs toilet isn't flushing right," Hannah explained, leading the way towards the stairs. Justin shot her a look of confusion. "Oh sorry, I forgot to mention it earlier, but I noticed it this morning."

He started to say something, but then thought better of it, clamping his mouth shut.

"Don't worry, I've already called someone to come take a look," Hannah added.

Lucy shifted her weight back and forth from one foot to the other, her need obviously urgent.

"Thanks babe!" Justin called. He watched as Hannah showed Lucy around the corner, pointing up the stairs so she would know where to go. He wished he had known about the downstairs toilet having an issue before having company over. He would have tried to fix it before they showed up.

"Should we play another round? Or do you want to wait for Lucy?" When no one protested, he drew a slip of paper.

"I've never gotten pregnant with my brother–in-laws' baby," Justin read and paused, flashing a glance at Lauren, the only one of them who was married with a baby.

At that moment, Hannah stepped back into the room. "What did I miss?" she asked, looking around at the rest of them, who were all staring silently at Lauren.

Justin just handed her the slip of paper, and she read silently to herself. He couldn't bear the thought of repeating it as he watched Lauren's expression go from shock to embarrassment.

Lauren's face puckered, looking like she was fighting off the urge to burst into tears.

Shit, I wanted to make everyone uncomfortable tonight, and talk about what happened, but not like this. Suddenly, Justin was filled with regret.

"What?" Alex asked, clearly trying to make sense of what was happening through his drunken stupor.

"I don't know," Lauren whispered and quickly swiped at a lone tear that fell.

Alex finally caught on. "Is that true? Is Cody... not Rich's?" His shock visible, he barely choked the words out.

"Wow, Lauren. That's a lot. Maybe we should take a break from this game," Hannah suggested, looking back down at the slip of paper in her hand. Justin looked at her, suddenly glad she was there tonight, even if it complicated things.

"Did you write that about yourself?" Nick whispered.

Lauren shot him a death glare. "Are you fucking kidding me? Do you think I would want one single soul to know my worst secret, my worst nightmare?"

"Your worst secret," Alex repeated.

Still not as bad as the secret pact we made in high school. Justin fought to keep the thought to himself.

"I'm going to go outside and have a smoke," he announced, pacing nervously around, looking for his pack of cigarettes.

"You smoke?" Alex asked, surprised.

Justin merely bobbed his head, still searching for his pack of cigarettes.

"Where's Lucy anyway? She's been gone a long time." Alex glanced towards the stairs.

"Probably hurling her guts up. She had way too much to drink," Nick guessed.

"I'll go check on her. I have to pee too anyway," Lauren offered, standing.

"The bathroom is at the top of the landing to the left. I'm going to just go take some of these empty plates to the kitchen." Hannah gestured and Lauren nodded, sliding past her and up the stairs.

"I need to make a phone call, I'm going to step outside for a minute too," Nick said, heading towards the hallway for the basket of phones.

"Ha!" Justin said, triumphantly holding up his cigarettes.

Alex stood up too. "Mind if I wander around a little, stretch my legs?" he asked.

"Yeah, no problem man. I'll be right back in." Justin turned and headed outside.

34

TWO YEARS BEFORE
GAME NIGHT

L auren stared at the paper in her hand, finally having her answer. Her whole world was about to crumble. She looked at the paper again, not wanting to have made any mistake.

The words blurred, and she swiped away tears.

"Probability of Paternity > 99.9999%," she read for what felt like the hundredth time.

She paced while she waited for Joel's call after texting him that the results were in. They had never discussed what would happen next if this was the result. Deny it? Lauren wasn't sure if she knew what she wanted. But knowing who Cody's father was made her long for a family that she didn't think could ever be.

Glancing over at Cody sleeping soundly in his little

swaddle, she clutched her phone in her hand. The screen lit up with the incoming call, and she jumped. She hit ANSWER and lifted the phone to her ear. "Hey–"

"Okay, Lauren, what was the result?" Joel cut her off, sounding like a different man than the one she'd been having an affair with for the past year.

"It's you. You're the father," Lauren said, not wanting to drag it out.

Joel swore, and Lauren flinched. As much as she knew they'd fucked up, she thought Joel loved her and that... maybe he might *want* Cody to be his.

"What are we going to do?" she whispered.

"No one can ever know, Lauren. This would destroy my marriage. Beth would never let me see Sammy. Rich would probably never speak to me again. It would destroy both of our families."

Lauren's heart dropped. She knew what he was saying was true, but somewhere in the back of her mind she had hoped he would say something else. Something about running away and raising their son together.

But... did she love Joel? Yes.

Maybe?

The more she thought about it, she realized she didn't. She had just seen it as a way to leave Rich. Not that there was anything wrong with Rich—he was a decent guy, a good husband, and was turning out to be a great dad. But she just wasn't in love with him. She was pretty sure now that she never had been.

"Lauren, did you hear me?" Joel broke into her thoughts, bringing her attention back to their call.

"Yes, sorry, I'm just... in shock still, I think."

"Right, so listen, we need to just pretend that what

happened between us *never* happened. Do you understand? And get rid of that paper. We need to focus on our
own marriages and our own kids." Joel was cold. Lauren
couldn't believe she'd actually thought he might be broken
up over this, that he'd been in love with her. She blinked
away tears, trying not to think about how she was taken
for a fool, how Joel had used her as a sex-toy for a year.
Until it had gone horribly, horribly wrong.

Looking down at Cody, she realized it hadn't gone
wrong. Not for her. She may not have wanted kids
anytime soon but now that Cody was here, he was her
world. Before him, it had seemed like nothing would ever
change, that she would always be alone. Sure, she had a
husband, but it hadn't been enough. Now, though, Cody
was the center of her universe.

She had been nothing more than convenient for Joel.
With no kids of her own, she'd been able to see him
whenever he slipped away from work. Rich had
commented in the past about Joel's wandering eye. She
wondered if he had other kids he'd written off.

"Consider it done," Lauren said, her tone as cold and
distant as she could muster. "See you at the next family
gathering." Lauren knew she sounded bitter. After all, why
wouldn't she be? He'd used her and when push came to
shove, he wanted to pretend they'd had nothing, shared
no real feelings.

Before Joel responded, she hung up and tore the paternity results into tiny bits and flushed them down the
toilet.

Rich was Cody's dad, in every sense but one—biology.
What other choice did she have?

35

SENIOR PARTY

Lucy and Alex fought all the way to his car. Nick and Lauren followed but lingered back. They'd all arrived together and would therefore leave together. Even though they'd taken Alex's car, Nick needed to drive since he was the only sober one, other than Justin. But Justin wasn't around. Still, Nick didn't want to push things and experience Alex's wrath.

"Alex, I'm sorry, but we haven't been getting along for months! This meant nothing," Lucy cried, and Nick flinched. "Our relationship has been over; we've both known it."

Nick wasn't sure if she meant it, but hearing he'd meant nothing to Lucy hurt. It was enough to trip him up and almost send spiraling, but he pushed those feelings down. Regardless of what he felt for Lucy, what they'd done was wrong. He claimed to be Alex's best friend, but he certainly hadn't acted like it. The remorse was there, but he wasn't sure if it was because of what they had done… or because they'd been caught.

"Well, I didn't know it. You were over our relationship? Then you should have ended it, Lucy. You should have. Because I was still in it," Alex rambled, stumbling over his own feet. They reached the vehicle, and Alex opened the driver's side door.

"What are you doing?" Lucy shrieked.

Nick's heart pounded, panic building. What was Alex thinking?

"Going home. You can get your own ride." Alex slid into the driver's seat and reached for the keys that Nick had left in the console.

"Dude, you can't drive!" Nick called, racing for the car. *I am such an idiot! Why did I leave the keys in the car?* Nick grabbed the door and held it open as Alex attempted to close it.

"Listen buddy, you're the last person I want to hear talking right now. Let go!" Alex wrenched the door out of Nick's hand and slammed it shut.

Nick jumped back, his fingers nearly smashed. Lucy raced around to the passenger side, yanking the door open and launching herself into the vehicle.

"Alex, don't be ridiculous, you can't drive," Lucy pleaded, reaching for the keys. Alex snatched them away from her and jammed the key into the ignition.

"I think I can do what I want. I'm a single man now, aren't I?" Alex scoffed.

"Alex, you can't drive!" Lauren yelled, pounding on the driver's side window.

Alex actually paused and looked at his sister. A twinge of relief flooded through Nick, thinking Alex would listen to reason. Nick hung back, hoping Alex would forget he was there, forget what had happened.

Alex exhaled and looked straight ahead. "I'm fine, Laur. Go back to the party. Find your boyfriend. Have fun." Alex started the car. Inside, Lucy screamed and burst into tears.

Nick paced next to the car, watching helplessly, not sure what to say that wouldn't make things worse. He wrung his fingers through his hair, not caring it stuck out and made him look like a madman.

"Please, Alex!" Lucy begged, desperation lacing her voice.

Nick's stomach ached.

"If you're getting out, get out now," Alex said, his voice cold. He nodded at the door.

"No, Alex. If you're going, I'm going with you. Please let's just talk about this," Lucy pleaded, mascara dripping down her face.

"Lucy, get out of the car!" Nick shouted.

Alex's laugh was dark. "You should listen to your boy toy." He put the car in drive. "Last chance," he warned. Lucy fastened her seatbelt as Alex revved the engine.

"Oh fuck, he's really leaving!" Nick's voice cracked.

Despite all the dumb pranks Alex had been so proud of over the last year, he'd never done anything so reckless. Never been so stupid.

While everyone else was wasted, Nick was sober. Of anyone, he should have been able to stop everything. It was all his fault. If Nick hadn't slept with Alex's girlfriend, he wouldn't be speeding away, drunk and wild with anger.

Nick realized what a shitty friend he'd been, but he didn't know how to rewind or fix it.

"Justin's car," Lauren suddenly said. "He always leaves the keys in the visor!" She raced towards her boyfriend's car and jumped into the passenger side as Nick slid into the driver seat, fumbling for the keys in the visor.

"Go, go, go!" Lauren shouted.

Nick peeled out, following Alex. Since Alex hadn't turned his lights on, it was hard to judge how far ahead he was, but as Nick drove over a small hill in the driveway, he saw Alex's SUV turn onto the road heading back into town.

Nick stepped on the gas. His heart raced, his fists gripping the wheel until his knuckles turned white. Stomach churning, dread filled every pore in his body.

36

SENIOR PARTY

ustin picked up his pace, running to catch up with Shane. The thick treeline loomed in front of them. If Shane got too far ahead, Justin would easily lose him in the dense woods.

"Shane, wait up, man!" Justin shouted, panting. Despite Justin's pleas, Shane's pace didn't slow. If anything, he sped up. The woods weren't far now, and Justin worried he'd never catch up.

Justin's eyes fought to adjust to the darkness. The trees seemed to swallow them. Any other time Justin would be freaked out about being out in the woods at night, but right now he couldn't process any fear other than the fear of Shane doing something stupid.

Justin forced himself to push harder, faster.

If he'd just refused to give Shane that pill... *What was*

even in that thing? It hadn't looked like the ones he'd usually grabbed, but he hadn't really thought about it.

This wasn't how Shane normally reacted to the pills. The opposite, in fact. Usually they made him chill, calm and relaxed. Justin's mind flicked back to the shot Shane had thrown back like it was nothing. *Could that one shot have interacted with the pill that much?* Of course the bottle said not to drink with it, but Justin couldn't believe that so little would make someone so irrational, like it flipped a switch.

Maybe this was just what had pushed Shane to the edge that he'd been dangerously close to. *I should have paid more attention to the pills I'd grabbed.* Justin had only glanced at the label, confirming it was marked as a narcotic pain killer. That had been all he needed to know.

Justin shoved down the guilt, focusing on trying to catch up to Shane.

It felt like an answered prayer when Shane's foot suddenly caught on a tree root and he tripped, falling to the ground with a heavy thud.

Catching up, Justin stood over Shane. "Are you okay?"

Shane groaned and rolled over, rubbing his elbow. Justin reached out to help him up, but Shane yanked himself away. He stood on his own and pushed past Justin. He limped but shook it off.

"I'm fine. Stop following me, okay? *Just stop following me!*" Shane's voice hitched, giving Justin pause.

If he listened and stopped following Shane, what would happen? What was the right thing to do?

Shane brushed the dirt and debris off his pants, wincing and cradling his elbow.

Justin bit his tongue, desperately wanting to urge him

back to the house. In the distance, Justin heard a car and realized they weren't that far from the road. Was Shane planning to run the entire way home? Justin's lungs were on fire, and he forced himself to breathe slowly. There'd be no way he could keep up if Shane kept going.

But then a terrifying realization hit him. On the other side of the road was a huge drop off. The cliff Shane had mentioned before.

A new fear blossomed in Justin's belly. Was *that* where Shane was headed?

For the first time, Justin wished he wasn't sober. That he didn't bear the responsibility of being the clear-headed one, because he still didn't know what to do. The weight of everything sat heavy on his shoulders.

"Don't follow me," Shane ordered, breaking Justin out of his thoughts. Shane turned and headed deeper into the woods. Justin ignored the command and jogged after him.

Shane began sprinting, leaping over fallen branches, darting around overgrown bushes. Justin fought to keep up. They neared the edge of the woods, and Justin sped up until he was just a couple of steps behind Shane. The light from the moon was barely enough to keep him from stumbling over his own feet.

The air around them was damp, as if it had just rained and the worms were overturning the dirt. Justin's shirt clung to him. He pulled it away from his sweaty chest, but there was no breeze. Every second felt like eternity. He bit back the bile from his stomach heaving.

Shane was focused, staring forward and running faster than Justin had ever seen him run. As they broke through to the other side of the woods, Justin saw headlights careening down the winding road.

Justin was only a few feet behind Shane. He lunged forward, trying to grab Shane before stepping out of the forest and onto the road. But he wasn't close enough.

His hand grabbed empty air as Shane's last leap landed him directly in front of the path of the SUV.

Too late.

37

GAME NIGHT

auren came back into the family room and found Justin sitting by himself. She paced back and forth, unable to sit still. Her mind was a tangled mess of thoughts.

"Lucy wasn't in the bathroom. You don't think she left, do you?" Lauren glanced towards the front door.

"No, everyone's car is still out front. I don't think she would drive drunk like that..." Justin's voice faded, and they looked at each other. Fortunately Nick returned, saving them more awkwardness. His face was bright red.

"Sorry, I wanted to clean up a little bit. Where's Alex and Lucy?" Hannah asked, coming back in from the kitchen.

"I don't know, Lucy wasn't in the bathroom," Lauren answered.

"Maybe they're hashing something out. Guess we should just let them have their moment," Justin suggested.

Unable to counter that, everyone just looked around at each other.

"Nick, why are you so red and sweaty?" Lauren asked, her nose wrinkling.

"Uh, just a phone call I had to make. Got me fired up." He forced a laugh, but Lauren didn't find his excuse believable. She doubted anyone else did either.

"I think I'm done drinking. And done with these games too." Lauren gestured towards the bowl, where a few slips of paper remained.

"How about a card game?" Justin asked, fidgeting as if nervous.

Nick's phone pinged and they all turned. Lauren was surprised he still had his phone, but the no phone rule didn't matter anymore.

His phone continued to ping repeatedly. Nick glanced around the room, uncomfortable. "It's Alicia. I should go back outside and give her a call," he said, sliding out of his chair and heading to the door.

"I think I'll take the rest of these cups back into the kitchen and bring out some bottles of water," Hannah offered. "Seems like everyone is done drinking. Maybe I should make some coffee?"

"Sounds good, babe. I need to use the bathroom." Justin hopped up and glanced at Lauren.

"I'll just wait here and see if Alex and Lucy come back down. I am starting to think they might have crashed in your bed upstairs." Lauren laughed, a hollow sound, but worry creased the lines around her eyes. When she caught her reflection in the window, she looked like she'd aged ten years in the course of the evening. Something was definitely not right, and everyone was tiptoeing around the elephant in the room.

"I'll check," Justin answered as he headed upstairs.

Lauren's mind flashed to Nick, wondering if he was really talking to Alicia. He'd seemed desperate to get away from everyone. And Justin was acting nervous, like he had something to hide. She shook the thought away. He was probably sweating bullets because he worried someone would spill the group's big secret in front of Hannah.

The tension in their shrinking party was vibrating like a live wire, crackling with something unknown that made the hair on the back of Lauren's neck stand up. Why did it feel like something was seriously wrong? They had spent years avoiding each other and now here they all were... Why? She couldn't even answer why *she* had decided to come.

The evening was getting out of control... but she'd had too much to drink to drive home yet. Desperate to escape, she realized she was stuck, at least for now.

38

GAME NIGHT

onestly, Lucy made it too easy to eliminate her. She didn't even put up that much of a fight, almost like she was grateful to have someone else end it for her. She had been slowly killing herself by starvation anyway. This was a mercy kill.

As she stepped out of the bathroom, I came up behind her and looped a stocking around her neck and pulled tight. She barely had time to let out a squeak. Her struggle against me was meek and lasted barely a minute. Then she made eye contact. I saw the confusion, and I relished in her fear. As I pulled the stocking tight, her eyes bulging, I reminded her of what she had done.

"You, being such a horny little slut, you set off everything that night. You were the catalyst to everything. But you all have to pay for Shane dying. I'm just sorry it's taken me so long."

Her fingers clawed at the stocking, but I pulled it tighter and wrestled her into the spare bedroom next to the bathroom.

"You could have prevented everything. Shane's death, what's going to happen tonight. It's all your fault," I raged.

She stared at me, questions swirling around that pretty little head as she struggled against me.

But then... she relaxed. Her hands dropped to her sides. I watched the life drain from her, her pupils losing focus, her mouth going slack. When she finally stilled, I gently lowered her to the floor.

I dragged her to the bedroom closet, opened the door, and shoved her in. She was so light. She couldn't have weighed more than 85 pounds. I closed the closet door and straightened up.

Thankfully there was a full length mirror in the room, and I adjusted myself in front of it, wiping the beads of sweat from my brow, and fixing my clothes before stepping out of the bedroom and silently pulling the door shut behind me. I stood on the landing for a few seconds before heading back downstairs to join the others.

39

SENIOR PARTY

The air inside the car was thick with tension. Alex beat his hand against the steering wheel, his eyes bloodshot, his movements jerky. Anger clenched his jaw so tightly it was a wonder he didn't chip his teeth.

Lucy sat beside him, her face blotchy and red from crying, her arms crossed tightly across her chest. She'd stopped begging him to slow down because it had only made him drive more erratically.

She tried another tactic. "You don't get to act like this, Alex," she said, her voice trembling. "You're drunk! You're out of control!"

Alex's grip tightened, his knuckles popping. *"I'm* out of control?" he slurred. *"I'm out of control?* You were the one who fucked my best friend! You think I'm supposed to just *forget* about that, Lucy?"

Her face contorted, guilt flashing in her eyes. "It didn't mean anything. You've got to believe me. I was—I was just confused. I—"

"Confused?" Alex's voice was low but seething. He slammed his foot down harder on the gas pedal. The car surged, and he nearly misjudged the curve in the road. The headlights sliced through the trees, but Alex was beyond caring about the road now.

"I'm the one who's confused, Lucy. I'm the one who doesn't understand how the hell you could do that to me. *To us.*"

Lucy shifted in her seat, bracing herself against the force of his driving. The car veered to the left, tires screeching, as Alex took another sharp curve way too fast.

"Alex, *please*, slow down. This isn't helping anything."

Alex didn't care. The alcohol burned in his veins, his anger boiling over in waves. "You think I don't see it? Huh? You think I didn't notice the way you two look at each other? You think I'm *blind*?"

Behind them, Justin's car followed at a distance, headlights gleaming in the rearview mirror. Nick had been trailing them ever since the fight started, watching them spiral from a safe distance, sober and silent.

Alex clenched his jaw. His hands shook as he gripped the wheel. "You don't get to tell me how to feel, Lucy! You *don't!*"

Lucy was quiet for a moment, her face etched with guilt. "I'm sorry… I'm so sorry, Alex. I was wrong. But this—this isn't you. You're not like this."

"You don't get to tell me who I am anymore either," Alex growled. He slammed his foot on the gas pedal. The car sped faster, the road twisted, the headlights flashing between trees. "You ruined everything. *Everything*. And now I'm the one who has to live with it."

Lucy reached over, her hand trembling as she grabbed his arm. "Please, Alex, stop. You're not thinking straight."

The car raced down the road, dark silhouettes of trees flying past them. Alex was spiraling, his heart hammering in his chest, blood rushing through his veins and thudding in his ears. He barely noticed the headlights behind them gaining on them.

Alex's eyes flickered between Lucy and the road, but before he could register the figure darting in front of them, a sickening *thud* echoed through the night.

The world spun.

His heart stopped.

Lucy screamed.

Tires screeched against the asphalt, and the car jerked to a stop, but it was too late.

The limp body lay broken and twisted at an unnatural angle where it had been tossed on impact. Justin burst out of the woods, skidding to a stop, his mouth open.

"Shane!" Justin screamed, racing over to Shane and dropping to his knees.

Through the cloud of smoke from his tires, Alex sat frozen, his mind struggling to process what happened. The world around him became distorted. Headlights behind them flashed, but he couldn't focus on anything other than the body in the road.

Lucy recovered first, gasping beside him. Her face was drained of all color when she turned toward him. "You—you—you hit him," she whispered before yelling, "Oh my God, Alex, you hit him!"

Alex couldn't move. He stared blankly while Justin felt

Shane's wrist and neck, clearly searching for a pulse. Justin's hands visibly shook, becoming more frantic until at last he fell back onto his ass. The pain in his eyes was unforgettable. He didn't speak. No one did. The silence was deafening and seemed to stretch a lifetime.

Finally, Justin pressed his hand to Shane's chest, tears streaming down his face.

"Call an ambulance," Lauren's voice cut through the silence as she climbed out of Justin's car. "We need help! Someone needs to call!"

Nick stepped out of his car, his face tight with disbelief. He stumbled towards Alex's car. He reached out to Alex who was still gripping the wheel, his breath ragged and erratic.

"We need to get out of here," Nick whispered, but Alex didn't respond.

Lucy's hands shook as she reached for Alex, her eyes wide with terror. "Alex, what have you done?"

Alex's mind was blank, his thoughts fractured. But one thing slowly became crystal clear: he had just killed someone. He had taken a life. There was no coming back from that.

The night air stilled, even the insects went mute. The only sounds were the panicked footsteps of people shuffling around Shane's lifeless body. The night seemed to stretch out forever.

The weight of reality crushed Alex. Their lives were shattered. How would any of them pick up the pieces and go on?

40

GAME NIGHT

knew Alex would be harder to kill. Honestly, I'd hoped he would be a little more drunk by the time it was his turn, but the opportunity presented itself, and I took it.

He was a big guy, towering over the rest of us. Because of that, I'd been the most worried about how it would go with him. I'd been counting on him being totally wasted, barely able to stand.

But here he was in the small office off of the den, snooping around. He wasn't the brightest guy, so his idea of snooping seemed to involve looking at the pictures and nicknacks on the shelves.

The office was tiny, barely room for the desk, short shelf, and one chair. As I hovered around the corner, I tried to envision how much space was needed before he dropped to the *ground. Time wasn't on my side. Everyone else was occupied now. I needed to hurry.*

My heart raced, and I tried to quiet my heavy breaths. Reaching into my pocket, I pulled out the needle I'd prepared, knowing I couldn't physically overpower Alex. It wasn't fair that the one person who was directly responsible for ending Shane's life was going to suffer the least, but it was the only way. Once injected, his heart would stop within minutes, but even before that, he wouldn't know what was going on. He'd be immobile, unable to call for help. I'd have to savor those seconds of sheer terror. Look him in the eye.

Silently, I pulled off the cap to the needle and adjusted the grip in my fist. I studied his neck, thankful he'd worn a collarless shirt. The biggest obstacle I could foresee was how to lower him to the floor without a sound.

No more stalling.

I crept forward, my feet landing softly on the carpet, and jammed the needle into his neck. Alex jerked his head in surprise, his eyes widening as he gaped at me. He stumbled and lifted his hand to the needle sticking out of his neck.

"That's for Shane," I whispered. He fell to his knees, the thick carpeting muffling the sound.

His mouth opened and closed like a fish out of water. His eyes searched my face for answers. I only smiled. Reaching forward, I helped push his body gently down to the ground and watched him take his last gurgling breath.

Satisfied the job was done, I slipped out of the office and pulled the door shut behind me. As the evening wound down, I was confident no one else would go in there, but it never hurt to be cautious. I hadn't expected Alex to end up there either, yet he had.

I scanned the basket of phones before tucking it into the coat closet. How convenient the "no cell phone" rule was turning out to be. It wouldn't be good if someone started wondering where everyone was going and found a body. I couldn't have them making a phone call before I could do away with them.

41

GAME NIGHT

Nick paced along the side of the house. I couldn't believe my luck. He could have stayed in the driveway near the cars, making this so much harder, but he'd wandered over to an area that was completely in shadow. A tall privacy fence ran along the side of the property, making it unlikely for a neighbor to see anything.

He was deep in conversation, his head moving aggressively. It was evident he was having a heated argument. I paused for a minute, curious who he was talking to.

"No, Alicia, I told you where I was and who I'm with. I've had too much to drink and can't drive yet." Nick sighed heavily, before responding. "No, I don't need you to come pick me up. Let's see how I feel in an hour." Their tiff continued, and I slipped behind one of the overgrown shrubs, inching my way closer.

The rocks beneath my feet crunched, and I froze. Nick stopped talking and looked around.

"Shh," Nick said into the phone, but by the way he pulled the phone away from his ear, it was clear Alicia was still yapping away into it. "I gotta go," he said and ended the call. "Hello?" He said into the darkness before laughing at himself. "I'm such an idiot. This night is creeping me out." He turned back towards the front door.

I stepped out just as he neared the shrubs. He jumped and laughed. "What are you doing out here? You scared the shit out of me..."

I sidestepped and moved behind him before he registered what was happening. I pulled the blade hard and fast across his throat, leaving him no time to struggle. A fountain of blood coated the hedges making me grateful for the long coat I'd slipped on.

Nick stumbled forward, his hands flailing at his neck. I gave him a hard shove. He reached out blindly to catch himself but fell through a gap between two shrubs with a hard thump. I tossed the knife in the hedges after him.

I stood waiting and watching while his body twitched, blood continuing to pump out faster than I realized possible. The smell of it filled the air and coated my nostrils. I glanced around, nervous for a moment. Finding no one, I looked down and realized he was sticking halfway out of the hedges. It wouldn't do to have anyone find him that way before the job was complete.

Nick was a small guy, but his dead weight made it quite an effort to drag him so he'd be fully concealed behind the hedges. Stripping off the coat, I shoved it in with him. I wadded up the thin gloves I'd worn, tossing it onto the pile, and then stared down at my shoes. I couldn't be sure I hadn't gotten any blood on them, but I had no choice but to hope for the best.

Back at the front door, I wiped the soles on the welcome mat before slipping back inside unseen. Game night was almost done.

42

SENIOR PARTY

The headlights cast long, distorted shadows across the road. As a heavy fog descended, the trees seemed to close in on them, suffocating any hope of clarity.

Shane's body lay still in the middle of the road, a grim reminder of how fragile life is, how everything can go wrong in the blink of an eye. The night air, thick with tension, carried the bitter scent of fear, sorrow, and regret.

Still unable to move, Alex sat in the driver's seat of his car, hands gripping the steering wheel, his knuckles pale. His mind was numb, his body trembling as the reality of what he had done slowly began to set in. Every breath felt like an eternity, each one colder than the last.

He couldn't bring himself to look at Lucy. Not yet. Not

when the silence between them sat heavy like a rock. Like a tombstone.

Lucy, too, hadn't moved. Her hands rested in her lap, her face pale and devoid of expression. She was staring straight ahead, her eyes unfocused. Her chest rose and fell in shallow breaths, but the tears had stopped. Now, there was only a quiet emptiness.

Justin stood by Shane's body, his hands at his sides, his gaze fixed on the lifeless figure. He hadn't said a word since the moment he realized Shane was gone. There was nothing to say. There was no hope. Just a quiet, all-consuming horror.

Nick and Lauren stood a few feet from the others, neither speaking. Nick's jaw was clenched so tight it looked like it might crack, his eyes hard and distant. Lauren's face was ashen, her arms wrapped tightly around herself as if trying to hold herself together.

Finally, Nick's raspy voice broke through the silence. "We can't call 911. We can't tell anyone."

Lauren gasped but apparently couldn't muster words to dispute him. No one else spoke.

Nick's words hung in the air, heavy and undeniable.

Alex eventually turned his head to Nick. Alcohol still fogged his mind, but it was unable to mask the sharp edge of panic. "What the hell do you mean?"

Nick took a slow, deliberate step forward, his gaze unwavering. "You hit him, Alex. You *killed* him," he said, his voice quiet but firm. "There's no coming back from that."

"I didn't—" Alex's words caught in his throat, but he stopped himself. He couldn't lie, not anymore. He *had* done this. His hands had taken a life. "What the hell do we do then, Nick? Just pretend like it didn't happen?"

Nick didn't flinch, and the weight of his words seemed to sink into everyone around him, making the air feel even thicker. "If we call 911, if anyone finds out, this whole thing's over. Our lives are over. We don't get to walk away from this. You know how this goes. They'll tie us all together. They'll tie us to it."

Lauren stepped forward, shaky but certain. "He's right. We don't get to walk away. We're all involved, whether we want to be or not. If anyone gets caught, if any of us says anything, it's over."

Alex recognized the regret thick in Lauren's voice. He closed his eyes, rubbing his face with his hands, the weight of their words crushing him. "So... what? We just leave him here? We just—"

"We leave him," Justin interrupted, his voice cracking. He looked at Alex, and for a moment, there was a flicker of anger in his eyes. It quickly faded, swallowed by grief. "We leave him. We leave this behind. No one knows. And we never speak of it again. Not to anyone."

A cold silence descended upon them. The decision had been made, and the gravity of it settled like a stone in their chests. There was no turning back. There was no bringing Shane back. He was dead. Shane was Justin's best friend. If Justin thought it was the right thing to do, how could any of them disagree?

"We don't even look back," Nick added, unwavering. "We drive away. All of us. And we never talk to each other again. Justin, you're the only other sober one, so you should drive Alex's car."

"Never talk again?" Lucy whispered, as if the idea of

cutting herself off from everything she had known was unbearable.

"Never," Lauren said, her voice like steel. "We can't keep this between us. Not even for a second longer. The moment we talk about it, the moment one of us opens our mouth, it all falls apart. This is the only way. No cops. No family. No friends. We erase it from our lives," she paused and took a deep breath, "and we pretend it never happened."

Alex caught her eye and he knew she would do this for him. Their family would never be the same otherwise.

A finality hung in the air. It was suffocating. Everyone knew what this meant. This wasn't just about Shane, or about the consequences of one night—it was about their lives. This was the end of everything they'd ever known. The end of their friendships, the end of their past.

"I hate this," Lucy muttered, her tone thick with emotion. "But… you're right. I don't see another choice."

Alex didn't know what to say. He hated it too. He hated them all. He hated himself the most. But as he looked around at his friends, his heart heavy with guilt and regret, he knew they were right. There was no other choice. If they didn't do this, if they didn't sever ties, the weight of this night would bury them. All of them.

"I don't want to live with this," Alex said, breaking under the strain. "But… I can't go to jail. What about my car?" His voice trembled.

"We can't," Nick agreed. "None of us can. As for your car, I know a guy."

Justin turned his back to them all, his face crumpling as he wiped his eyes. "I just want it to be over."

The group waited in the silence that followed. The

weight of their pact settled like an anchor tied around each of their necks, grounding them to this moment in time. No one spoke again; they all understood. This wasn't just about what they had done. It was about the choice they made—to erase it all, to erase *each other*.

They would leave Shane there, in the middle of the road. They would drive off, their lives splintering in every direction. No goodbyes. No apologies. Just a silent pact that would bind them together in a different kind of way.

It was the only way to survive.

Without another word, they all turned away. Alex crawled over the console into the backseat, and Justin slid behind the wheel. The engines caught, a final hum in the night. They drove into the darkness, leaving their past and each other behind.

Never to speak again. **No matter what**.

43

GAME NIGHT

t felt like she'd been waiting forever for everyone to return, so Lauren got up and wandered into the kitchen. Hannah was standing at the sink, washing her hands.

"Can I do anything to help?" Lauren asked.

Hannah jumped. "Oh my gosh, you scared me!" Hannah raised a wet hand to her chest.

Lauren offered an apologetic smile. "Sorry about that, I just figured I'd help get the coffee." Lauren gestured towards the coffee maker sitting on the counter and saw that Hannah hadn't started it yet.

"Oh yeah, I was just cleaning up a few of the glasses and plates. I think I had a bit too much to drink and zoned out."

Hannah's titter grated on Lauren's nerves. She hadn't

seen Hannah drink that much but figured she was probably just taking a break from the group's drama. She couldn't imagine how awkward it was being the odd one out when the rest of them were obviously keeping such dark secrets.

"I can relate. I haven't had this much to drink since… well, probably ever." Lauren shook her head, desperate for that coffee now.

"Why don't you just have a seat, and I'll get the coffee going." Hannah gestured to the small kitchen table.

Lauren didn't hesitate to slump into one of the chairs, the weight of the night hitting her all at once. *Now everyone knows about Cody. They probably think I'm the shittiest wife. Who sleeps with their husband's brother?* Lauren tried to shake the brain fog. She didn't realize she'd had that much. *And here I insisted on driving Alex. Now we're both going to have to take an Uber home.*

"There you are!" Justin said, joining them in the kitchen. "Did Nick come back in yet?"

"No, his fiance must really be ripping him a new one." Lauren laughed dryly, and when Justin looked at her, surprised, she laughed again, and then set her forehead down on the table. Even she knew that her snarky comment was out of character. *Why do I feel like this?* She tried to remember how many drinks she'd had.

"You don't look so good. Coffee is almost ready," Hannah said, and Lauren glanced up as she pulled a mug down off the rack on the wall. She rested her head back down on the table, feeling so grateful no one was expecting her to do anything.

"Here you go," Hannah said, setting the full mug down in front of Lauren.

Lauren looked at the mug, her vision blurry. She wrinkled her nose, it was awfully dark. She liked a little coffee with her cream and sugar.

"Let me get you some milk and sugar," Justin offered, bringing the mug back over to the counter and sweetening Lauren's coffee for her, giving it a good stir. Setting it back down near her, Lauren lifted her head and nodded, reaching for it and taking a sip.

"Here's one for you too." Hannah set another mug down at the table for Justin.

He gave her a grateful smile and sank into the chair across from Lauren and reached for the hot mug. Hannah turned back to the coffee pot to make one more for herself and carried it over to the table.

"This has been a weird night, huh?" Hannah said, taking a delicate sip.

"Fuck, that's an understatement," Lauren said, taking a long drink, ignoring the burn as it went down. She needed to feel less drunk, now. The burn almost felt good, reinvigorating her senses and making her feel less numb.

Justin took a much more cautious sip and set the mug down to cool. Lauren kept at it until it was more than half gone. But… her head wasn't feeling any clearer.

Resting her forehead on the table again, she tried to calm the jitters in her stomach. Something felt terribly wrong. Lifting her head up again, her vision swam. Justin and Hannah were just two blurs in front of her. Or four blurs….

She blinked rapidly and tried to bring them into focus.

"Something doesn't feel right." The words garbled, her tongue thick.

"What?" Justin's forehead wrinkled. "Are you okay?

Maybe we should get you some water." Justin lifted his mug and took a long gulp. From the corner of his eye, he watched as Hannah sipped at her coffee, too.

"I feel worse," she tried to tell them. The room swayed and she saw dark spots.

She felt herself slipping away.

Just before her head slammed into the table, she had a moment of clarity.

The coffee had been laced with something.

44

GAME NIGHT

S hane never got to see adulthood. His life was cut short, ripped out of my life. Shane wasn't given the chance to learn that life could be better. And this group was the reason.

Everyone needed to get what they deserved. Shane was the closest person to me, my best friend, the one person I could always count on. The one I expected to become an adult with, to be reminiscing with until we were old and gray.

I'd been forced to learn how to live without him. Poisoning Lauren's coffee had been too easy. I wasn't sure how I was going to do that unnoticed, but it turned out to be so simple. I didn't know she would drink it so quickly, but that was just an added bonus. I'd tried to plan everything as meticulously as I could, but honestly, some things I had to leave up to fate.

For a moment, I reflected on how Lauren and Lucy had both

denied their infatuation with each other. How they'd cheated on their male partners with other men. Lucy, I could understand. She had always been so worried about what other people thought. Lauren was more complex. I wish I'd been able to ask her more about that before she died, but I'd made peace with knowing I wouldn't get all the answers. I had to carefully follow my timeline, or everyone's growing suspicion would turn against me.

The night was moving along smoothly. There was just one loose end to tie up.

Then I would clean up my mess and disappear.

45

GAME NIGHT

Justin jumped out of his chair as Lauren's head hit the table. Hannah jerked back, her coffee sloshing over her mug.

"Oh gosh, she's really drunk, huh?" Hannah asked, looking over at Lauren.

"More than a little," Justin muttered. He took her mug and set it in the sink before turning the water on to rinse it.

"Where is everyone else?" Hannah asked.

Justin, who was facing away from her, paused. His shoulders rose in a tense shrug. "That's a good question. It's weird, right?" Justin asked, his words slurring.

Hannah nodded. Justin turned back to face her. He moved his mouth around, smacking his lips together. His nose scrunched up.

"My tongue feels thick." Confused, he looked at Hannah.

A slow smile spread across her face.

"What's funny?" he asked, annoyed. It sounded like he had marbles in his mouth.

"Should we finish playing 'Never Have I Ever?'" she asked.

He blinked, reaching for his chair and stumbling into it. "I don't feel right. What the fuck, Hannah? Why would we play that stupid game?" Justin fumbled with the words, saliva sputtering out with each movement of his mouth. Even he realized that what he was saying was incomprehensible, but Hannah didn't look concerned.

He reached for his mouth, wanting to know why his tongue wasn't working right, and why he suddenly felt so drunk. He held the table to steady himself.

Hannah sighed and rolled her eyes. She stood up and walked over to the counter. "You're being kind of dramatic, aren't you?"

She stopped in front of the knife block, slowly sliding out the biggest knife. Looking at the blade, she smiled again and turned back to Justin who was staring at her, blinking to clear his vision.

"What are you doing?" he asked.

She stepped closer to the table and laughed.

46

Hannah sat on the edge of the couch, legs tucked underneath her, as she scrolled through her phone. The soft hum of the apartment's quiet evening was broken only by the sound of an occasional car driving by. She glanced at Justin leaning against the kitchen counter, his eyes distant as he stared into his coffee cup.

He'd been like this for the past few days—quiet, withdrawn, like he was a million miles away. Ever since running into his old friends, it was as though his thoughts had been focused on nothing else.

She cleared her throat, trying to bring a little cheer into the conversation. "Hey, I was thinking... we should have a game night this weekend."

Justin raised an eyebrow. "A game night?" he repeated, his voice flat. "With who?"

"Well," she said, her voice light, "I was thinking you could invite some old friends. You know, the ones from high school. You said you ran into a couple recently that you hadn't seen in forever."

Justin hesitated. "I don't know, Hannah. It's been a long time since I saw those guys. I'm not really in the mood to relive all that, you know?"

Hannah bit her lip, considering her next words carefully. "I get it. But, you know, you used to love playing games, right? I bet you were really competitive."

A shadow passed over his face, but it vanished just as quickly. "Yeah, I guess... but wait, how did you know that?" he mumbled. "That was a long time ago. High school was a different time."

Hannah nodded, her voice softening as she stood up and walked over to him. She reached out and gently touched his arm, her fingers brushing against the fabric of his sleeve.

"I was cleaning out the cabinets and ran across a stack of old games. I assumed you must have been big into them at some point. But they didn't look like they'd been touched in years." She smiled, a glint of mischief in her eyes.

Justin stiffened. "I don't... I didn't know I still had those."

"You don't remember putting them in there?" she asked, but quickly added, "No matter. It just made me think, why not have a game night? That's a thing, right? It'd be such a great way to catch up with old friends.

Surely you have other friends from high school you could invite? Then no one would feel out of place."

Justin was quiet. She saw the flicker of temptation in his eyes. But the pain from the past still clung to him, a dark cloud following him everywhere.

"I'm not sure that's a good idea, Hannah," he said, softer. "I'm rusty. I haven't played in years."

"Exactly!" she said, nudging him gently. "It'll be fun. And you'll get to catch up with all your old friends."

Justin let out a quiet, reluctant laugh.

"Let's do it next Friday night!" Hannah said, excited. "You ran into, what was it, Alex and Nick? Did I get those names right? Who else were you close to in high school?"

His eyes darkened before he blinked it away. She stepped back and clapped her hands together as though she were finalizing a deal. "Come on, what do you say? Game night next weekend. Just a few of us. It'll be fun. I'll make food and drinks—make it a proper night in."

Justin hesitated but then, with a deep sigh, he gave her a resigned smile. "Alright, alright. You win. I'll do it. But you're *definitely* going down!"

Hannah's heart skipped a beat, the anticipation keeping her grin wide. "That's the spirit! Who else will you invite?"

"Um, I mean, Alex had a sister, Lauren. But I dated her for a while in high school. Would that be too weird?"

"Of course not, silly! High school was ages ago!" Hannah waved off his concern.

"Then probably Lauren's best friend too, Lucy," Justin said. His guarded tone made her worry he was wondering what sort of mistake he was making. She had to keep the excitement up but also within reason.

"Oh babe, that sounds great. Just the six of us then, perfect number!" Hannah hopped up. "Reach out to them now!" She bounced out of the room, and Justin sat, clutching his phone.

47

GAME NIGHT

"Are you feeling a bit... woozy, Justin? I made that coffee special for Lauren, you know, but I'm so glad you had some, too," Hannah said, stepping closer to him as he hunched over the table.

"Hannah? What the fuck is going on?" The words were like mush in his mouth.

"It's not Hannah." Her smile slipped but she forced it back. "Justin, do you remember your stepdad? Good old Coach Troy?" Hannah stood next to the table, turning the knife over and over in her hands, studying her reflection in the shiny blade.

"Wha... What?" Justin tried to get out of his seat but had to grip the back of it for balance.

"Do you really think the pills that you gave Shane aren't the reason he's dead?"

Shock washed over Justin's face, confusion wrinkling his forehead.

"He wasn't supposed to drink, Hannah! I didn't know what would happen!" Justin cried, his voice catching, the years of guilt flooding him. His eyes followed the knife in her hand.

"I'm not Hannah!" she screamed.

"Then who are you?" Justin's voice wobbled.

"You really don't know, do you? Never suspected. Your friends are all dead by the way. Lauren isn't just passed out. She's dead. Alex, dead. Lucy, dead. Nick," she said, inching closer, "dead. And you're next, Justin." She watched as he sifted through things, trying to figure it out.

Heaving a loud sigh when she realized he couldn't, she took another step closer and poked the tip of the blade into the side of his neck.

Justin flung himself back and tried not to fall out of his chair. "Just stop, put the knife down, Hannah... or whoever you are," Justin slurred.

This is going to be an easy fight. "Sloane. My name is Sloane. And Shane was my brother," she said.

Justin froze.

"You all killed my brother and walked away with nothing to show for it."

"Nothing to show for it?" he spat. "Couldn't you tell how the guilt ate all of us alive? It's been ruining our lives for ten years. Worse than prison." His words jumbled together, and he staggered.

"You all are the reason Shane is dead! And you, Justin, you knew what Coach Troy did, didn't you? To me? I saw you that day. You could have helped me. You could have said something. But you were more worried about yourself. I swapped out those pills. Pills I'd seen the coach take many, many times. But I had no idea someone else would come along and swipe them like a common criminal. Especially," she seethed, "not someone who was going to give them to my brother."

She paused and paced, gathering memories. "I was just there for a special athletic program. For some reason Coach Troy targeted me. And then threatened me if I ever told. I wanted to make him pay, but *you* took that away! Just like you and your fucking friends took Shane away. You stole *everything* from me! You ruined my life!" Sloane screamed, breathing hard.

She closed her eyes and took some meditative breaths. When she opened them and looked at Justin, an eerie calm replaced all emotion.

"Thanks for having me here the last couple of months. It's been helpful." Sloane smiled, but it didn't reach her eyes.

A bit of regret crossed her mind as she plunged the knife into Justin's chest. Of all of them, Justin had loved Shane like a brother. She knew his role in what had happened were horrible mistakes made by an immature kid. But he still hadn't taken responsibility. He was part of the problem. If nothing else, he'd served his purpose.

48

FOUR MONTHS AFTER
SENIOR PARTY

Hazel slammed her locker shut. Nerves danced in her belly. Given the fact that Shane had been a year ahead of her, she knew she'd have to face her senior year without him. But now that school was back in session, the reality of why he wasn't there hit her like a freight train.

Summer had been miserable. She'd spent most of her days working at the local bowling alley, which had left her little time to sit around and mope.

From the corner of her eye, she noticed Shane's sister opening her locker, her hair curtained around her face.

So, the rumors were true then. She didn't go back to boarding school.

Hazel heard that Shane's mother had freaked out and

wouldn't let her leave. Even though they were in the same grade, Hazel had never actually spoken to her. By the time Hazel had transferred to this school, Sloane had already been sent off to the boarding school. Shane had always told Hazel that Sloane wasn't just a gaming nerd; she was a real genius. She knew how to program and create elaborate games.

"Hey, I don't know if you remember me," Hazel said, stepping over.

"Yeah, you're... I mean, you *were* Shane's girlfriend, right?" Sloane's face was a blank slate, unreadable. "Hazel?"

Hazel beamed, pleased that she remembered from their brief encounters.

"So you're back here for senior year, huh? I can't wait until it's over." Hazel blew air out to get her bangs out of her eyes.

Sloane nodded but didn't say anything.

"What homeroom are you in?" Hazel asked, leaning against the lockers, pressing her notebook to her chest.

Sloane tossed her jacket into her locker and slammed the door shut, turning to face Hazel. "Mr. Morgan's." She didn't offer anything else.

Hazel forced her frustration down. Why was Sloane making this so difficult? It made sense that they should be friends, didn't it? They both loved and missed Shane, right? And neither had any other real friends here.

"Me too." Hazel forced herself to chill. "Do you want to walk up together?" Sloane shrugged but turned to follow Hazel's lead.

"It's weird to be here without Shane. It must be really

weird for you," Hazel said, testing the waters. She watched Sloane from the corner of her eye.

"I'm not even supposed to be here," Sloane muttered.

Hazel couldn't think of anything else to say, so they continued to homeroom in silence. Sloane might be a tough nut to crack, but Hazel was determined to be friends. She would just have to keep trying. Eventually Sloane would cave.

49

GAME NIGHT
TWO HOURS AFTER

azel watched the clock, waiting for Sloane to return. She was trying to be patient. After all, Sloane had to dispose of all the evidence of her temporary life. But Hazel was desperate to know if everything had gone as planned.

Looking at the clock again, she let her shoulders relax. It was almost 3:00 a.m. Any time now, she'd have answers. According to the plan, Sloane was expected back soon. That was if she hadn't run into any real issues.

When someone is responsible for killing the only person you'd ever loved, you just don't get over it. Ten years later, both Hazel and Sloane realized they'd never be able to move forward. Hazel had had no one else back then. Her dad had run off when she was still in diapers, and her mother... well, she could barely call her that.

Shane had saved her. Without him, she wouldn't have made it through high school. When he died, her whole world collapsed. It had seemed natural to get closer to his sister.

Hazel and Sloane became close after Shane died. In fact, both of them excluded everyone else from their little world. As they grew closer and their friendship turned into more, Sloane revealed what had happened. Up until then, Hazel hadn't known who was responsible. Much like everyone else, she'd thought it was someone from out of town and that the case would never be solved.

But Sloane had seen everything that night. She had watched in horror as Justin chased after her brother. Desperate to know what was going on, she'd taken a shortcut through the woods, racing around a cluster of trees. From the opposite side of the road, she'd witnessed everything. Alex's car. Shane's body flying like a ragdoll through the air. The screeching tires. The silence that followed.

She'd screamed but the sound was swallowed by the night. No one noticed her as her knees buckled, and she crumbled to the ground. Frozen in place, unable to move, the others' frantic voices carried to her. Then Nick's cut through the rest of them. "He's dead."

Sloane had turned and thrown up, her legs shaking too violently to stand back up.

Fumbling around, she'd searched for her cell phone. In a panic, she realized it was in Shane's car, abandoned when they'd arrived at the party.

She remained crouched in the woods long after

everyone else had made their pact not to tell anyone. She had heard it all. Then they'd climbed back in their cars and sped off, leaving Shane's dead body in the middle of the road.

They'd almost been caught. Not long after they'd left, a car came along. They'd slammed on their brakes, narrowly missing Shane. That's who called 911 that night. Not Alex, Lucy, Justin, Nick or Lauren. And not Sloane.

Sloane had stayed hidden, watching the scene unfold as the stranger called for help. It wasn't until after she'd made her way back to the party and found her cell phone in Shane's car that she broke down.

When she told Hazel, she was met with disbelief at first. Then anger. The same sort of rage that had been consuming Sloane all these long years. Hazel couldn't let them get away with it.

Hazel had slowly started planting little seeds until Sloane wanted what Hazel had always wanted.

Revenge.

This night was the culmination of years of planning and plotting and manipulating Sloane into thinking she was the right person to play the role.

Killing Coach Troy had been Hazel's gift to Sloane, to show her she meant everything she said. But it hadn't been as clean as she had wanted. It was fortunate that he had so much dirty laundry, because after his death, numerous people spoke about his character, making it clear he had a lot of enemies. It seemed even the cops didn't invest as much into the case as they would have otherwise.

Hazel heard a key in the front door. Her pulse sped up, and she prepared herself for the news—good or bad.

"Hazel?" Sloane called, her voice breaking.

Hazel rushed to greet her at the front door, clearing her face of any emotion so she could watch and match Sloane's. Sloane dropped a box on the floor, but Hazel paid little attention to it.

Sirens blared in the background, growing closer.

"What happened?" Hazel asked, suddenly concerned as the crunch of tires in the driveway drew her eyes over Sloane's shoulder.

"What have you done?" Sloane cried out as the police beat rushed forward.

"What are you talking about?" Hazel backed away from her.

"How could you?" Sloane shouted dramatically, pushing away from her as the police burst in.

Hazel froze. *What is she doing?* Her mind raced as their condo flooded with activity.

"She's right here!" Sloane cried, pointing at Hazel.

Mute with confusion, Hazel stared open-mouthed as police surrounded her. Staring at Sloane, unable to speak, she could only wonder *what had she done?*

50

GAME OVER

Game Night was the most important game I'd ever played. All along, Hazel had thought I was her pawn. Little did she know what I was capable of. I trusted no one.

It was easy enough to plant clues at the scene leading back to Hazel. It was also easy enough to bring home a box of evidence and call the police claiming she'd just confessed everything to me. The bloody knife laying inside the box was enough to scare me into calling the police immediately. At least, that's what I'd told them.

From the moment Justin walked in on Coach Troy molesting me and didn't stop him, I wanted him to pay. When I found out I wasn't the only girl the coach had assaulted, I replaced the pills with something much stronger. How could I have known Justin would take them, let alone give one to my brother?

After the night of the senior party, I was destroyed. Maybe I'd had a hand in it too, but not as much as them. And I could make everyone else pay. I'd already started plotting before Hazel and I became friends. It'd been so easy. She was already a head case. And then when I revealed what I had seen and that I'd been too scared to report, Hazel let it slip that she had given Shane a couple of shots that night. So she had played a part too. I couldn't forgive myself for switching out the pills, but in the grand scheme of things, that paled in comparison to the roles everyone else played.

Originally, I wanted it to be her to do the dirty work. But as I got to know her, I realized that Hazel was great at planning, stalking, watching, and getting information. But when it came to action, she was clumsy, indecisive, and weak. She would make mistakes.

Her little display with Coach Troy had only proved me right. Her misguided attempt to show me how much she cared about me, how I could trust her, had been nothing short of a ploy to manipulate me. She'd gotten lucky when she got away with that murder, and while I could have stepped back and let her get caught for this night too, I was worried she would take me down with her. Or worse, fail in the middle of the job. I couldn't trust her to finish it without one or more of them figuring it out and stopping her.

I had to change my plan. I couldn't trust anyone else to do the dirty work and keep me from being implicated. No trace could be left behind. For months, I'd lived a double life. Hazel though: I'd taken a leave of absence from my job, but instead I had been traveling back and forth, lying to both Justin and Hazel about work.

When she tried to plead her innocence or share the blame with me, every explanation she had would fall short. Every piece of evidence would lead back to her. I had wiped the place clean of my fingerprints and made sure to leave hers behind. Her hairbrush, toothbrush, more of her personal possessions. Things she didn't even know I'd taken.

I'd played my best game, and now... who knew what else I was capable of?

ABOUT THE AUTHOR

This is Sara Lea's sixth book. She has also written two short stories. You can sign up to receive her newsletter by going to saraleabooks.com

www.ingramcontent.com/pod-product-compliance
Lightning Source LLC
Chambersburg PA
CBHW020409210626
46816CB00006BB/2199